MCR

J
Paris. M

Marty Pants

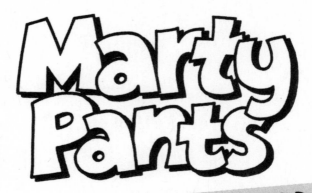

HOW TO DEFEAT A WIZARD

Also by Mark Parisi

MARTY PANTS #1: DO NOT OPEN!

MARTY PANTS #2: KEEP YOUR PAWS OFF!

HOW TO DEFEAT A WIZARD

Mark Parisi

HARPER
An Imprint of HarperCollins*Publishers*

To Lynn

Marty Pants #3: How to Defeat a Wizard
Copyright © 2018 by Mark Parisi
www.harpercollinschildrens.com
Library of Congress Control Number: 2017959287
ISBN 978-0-06-242780-9
Typography by Joe Merkel
18 19 20 21 22   CG/LSCH   10 9 8 7 6 5 4 3 2 1
❖
First Edition

DO WEIRD THINGS KEEP HAPPENING TO YOU?

OR IS IT JUST ME?

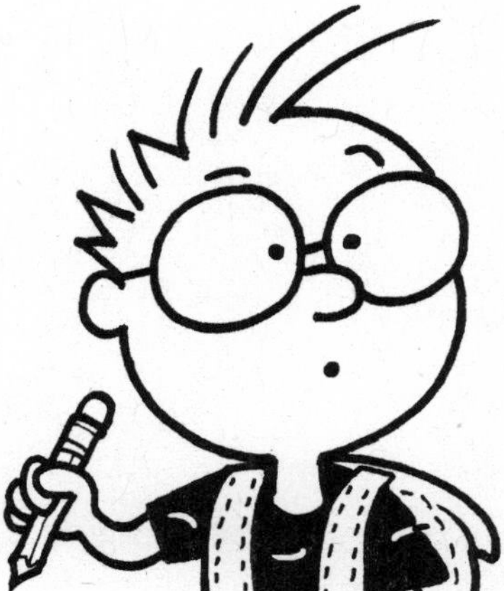

CHAPTER 0

teaser

I'm about to do something really crazy. I don't want to, I have to!

The end of civilization is about to go down, and I have to warn everyone! I think I have the courage to do what needs to be done, but I certainly can't do this alone.

Gurk! It may already be too late! The earth is starting to shake!

You know what? I should tell this story from the beginning, when this whole mess started.

It was a Tuesday.

CHAPTER 1
sorry not sorry

Apologize to Simon?

I can think of a few things I'd rather do than apologize to Simon.

1. Run naked through a cactus patch. (Without sunscreen.)

2. Eat a raw porcupine. (Without ketchup.)*

* Or catsup.

3. Listen to my dad talk about old music. (Without a pillow.)

But Principal Cricklewood isn't impressed with any of these options. She *insists* I apologize to Simon.

For what?

All I did was call Simon a

And I'm not even sure what it means. I just like the way it sounds.

I tried to explain to Principal Cricklewood that being called a monkey washer could be a compliment.

But something she said gave me the impression she wasn't buying it.

It's not fair. Simon insults me all the time but gets away with it because he's sneaky. He tricks people.

Even my mom falls for it.

A lot of people call Simon charming.

Charming, charming, charming.

I'm sick of hearing it.

Just for kicks, I hop on my dad's computer and look up *charming* to see if there's any possible definition that could apply to Simon.

TAP TAP TAP

charm-ing:

1. delightful, pleasant, likable, adorable

Ugh! Stop!

Simon is so *not* charming. How has he tricked people into thinking he's charming?

Hold on. There's a second definition.

charm-ing:

2. the act of using magic powers

CHAPTER 2

charmed, i'm sure

Whoa.

Could Simon have *magic powers*?

Is he literally a *charmer* who is *charming* people with magic *charms*?

No way. I'm very observant, and if that monkey washer had magic powers, I'd have noticed.

Definitely.

I'm a world-class noticer.

But then again, it sure would explain a few things.

1. Like why Simon's popular at school, even though he has this quality:

2. How Simon always gets away with tormenting me. Even as far back as kindergarten.

3. And most of all, why Simon is considered the school artist when it should rightfully be *me*!

Simon's not a true artist like I am. He's a poser who only draws one thing. ONE THING!

That's right. All he does is draw the famous character AnemoneBob TrapezoidShorts.* He draws it over and over and over and over, and everyone loves him for it.

* Can you figure out the real character I mean? Of course you can.

You know what? I don't want to think about the possibility of Simon having magic powers. That's too scary.

Almost as scary as having to write an apology to Simon for calling him a

MONKEY WASHER!

And I have to finish it by tomorrow. I better get started.

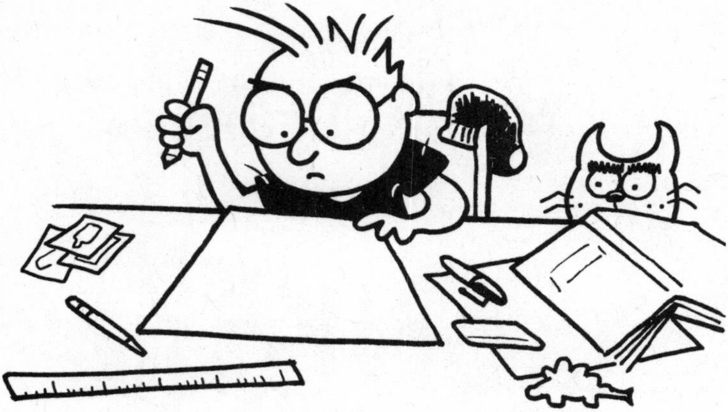

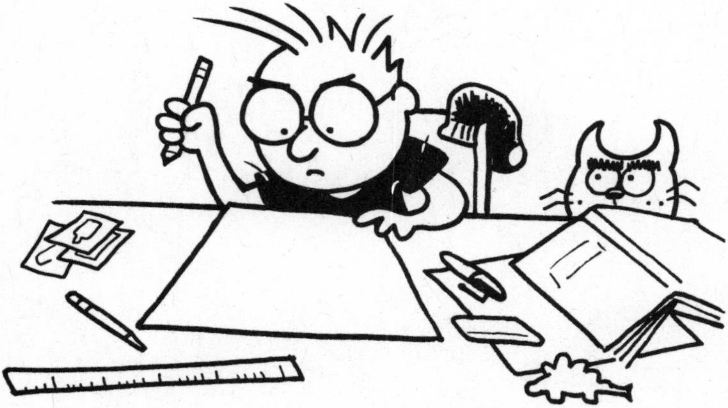

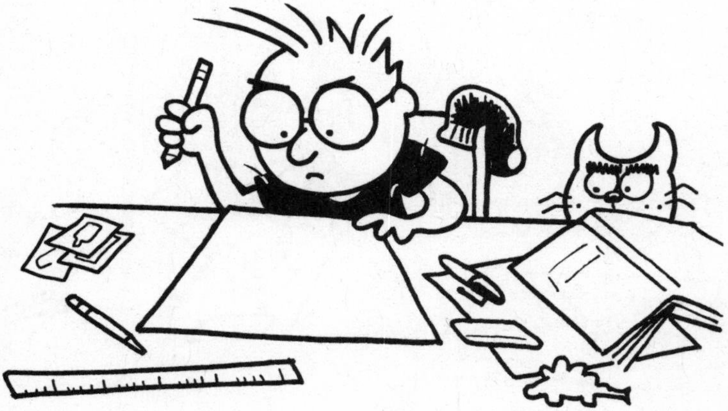

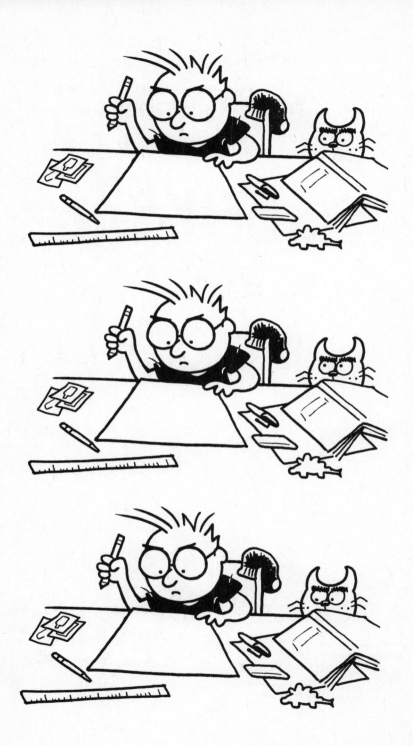

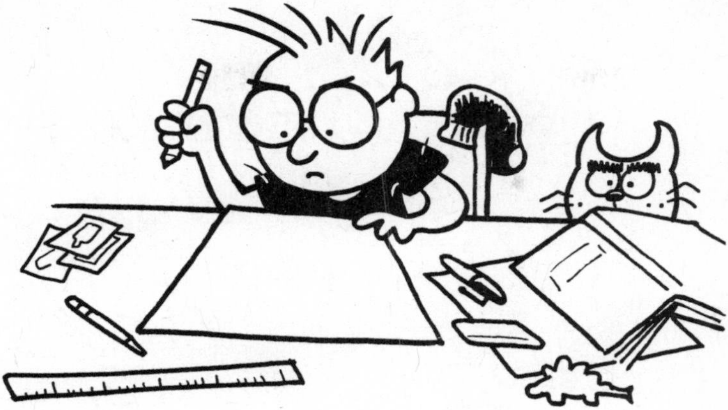

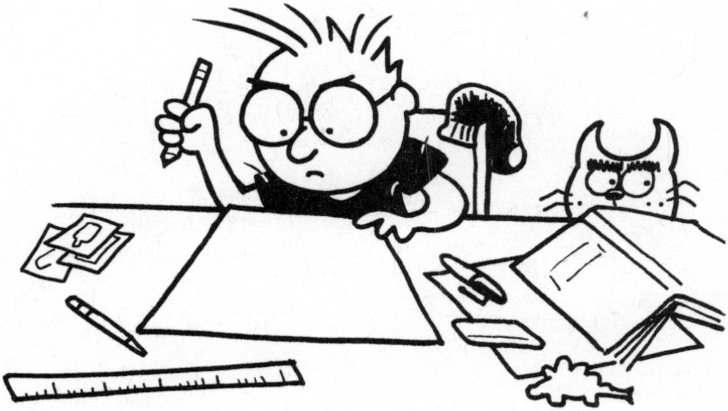

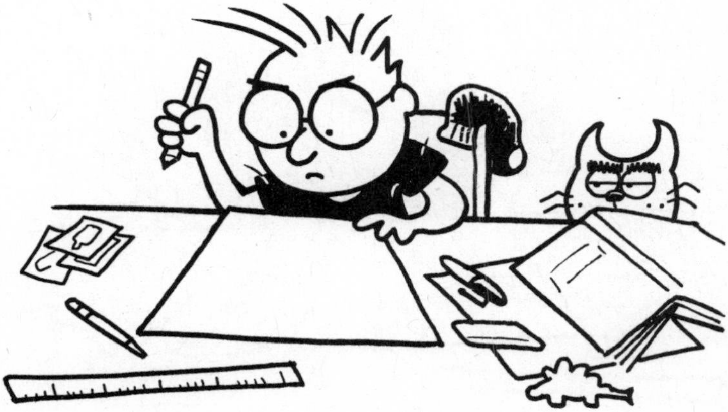

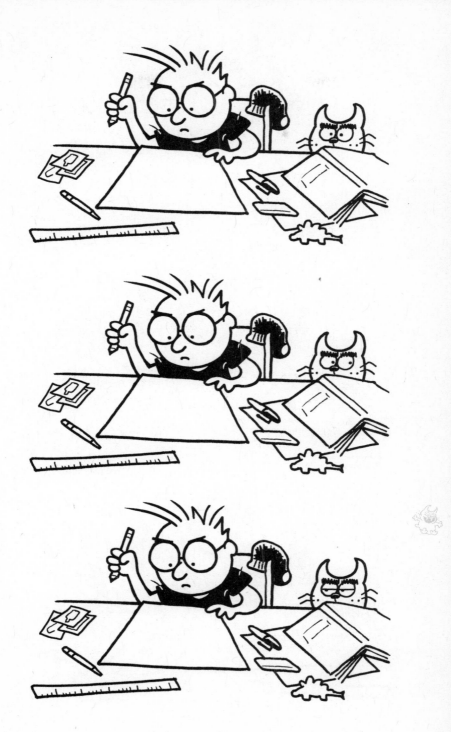

CHAPTER 3

nothing to see here

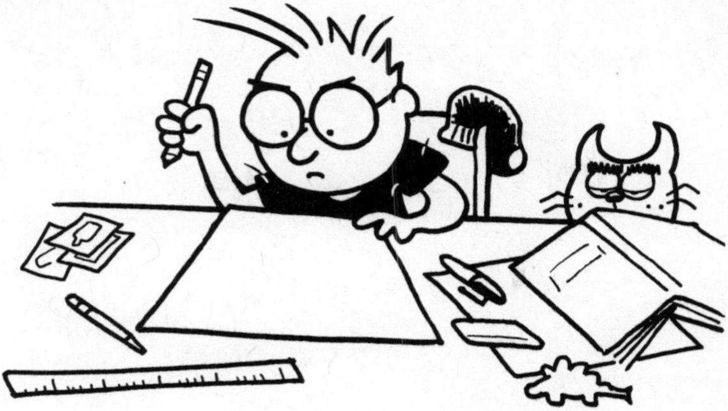

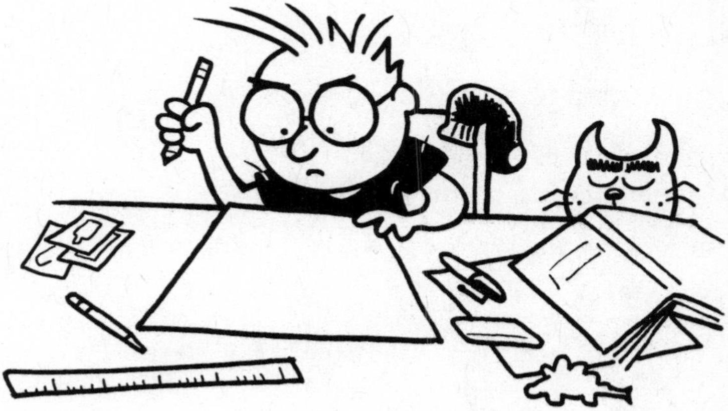

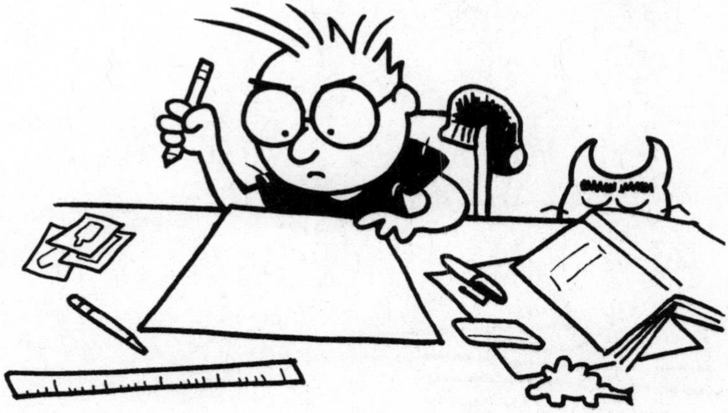

I can't seem to write this apology.

I must have a case of writer's block.

Maybe I should try writing something else first.

Something fun.

Something awesome.

Something to soothe my tortured, artistic soul.

HEH, HEH.

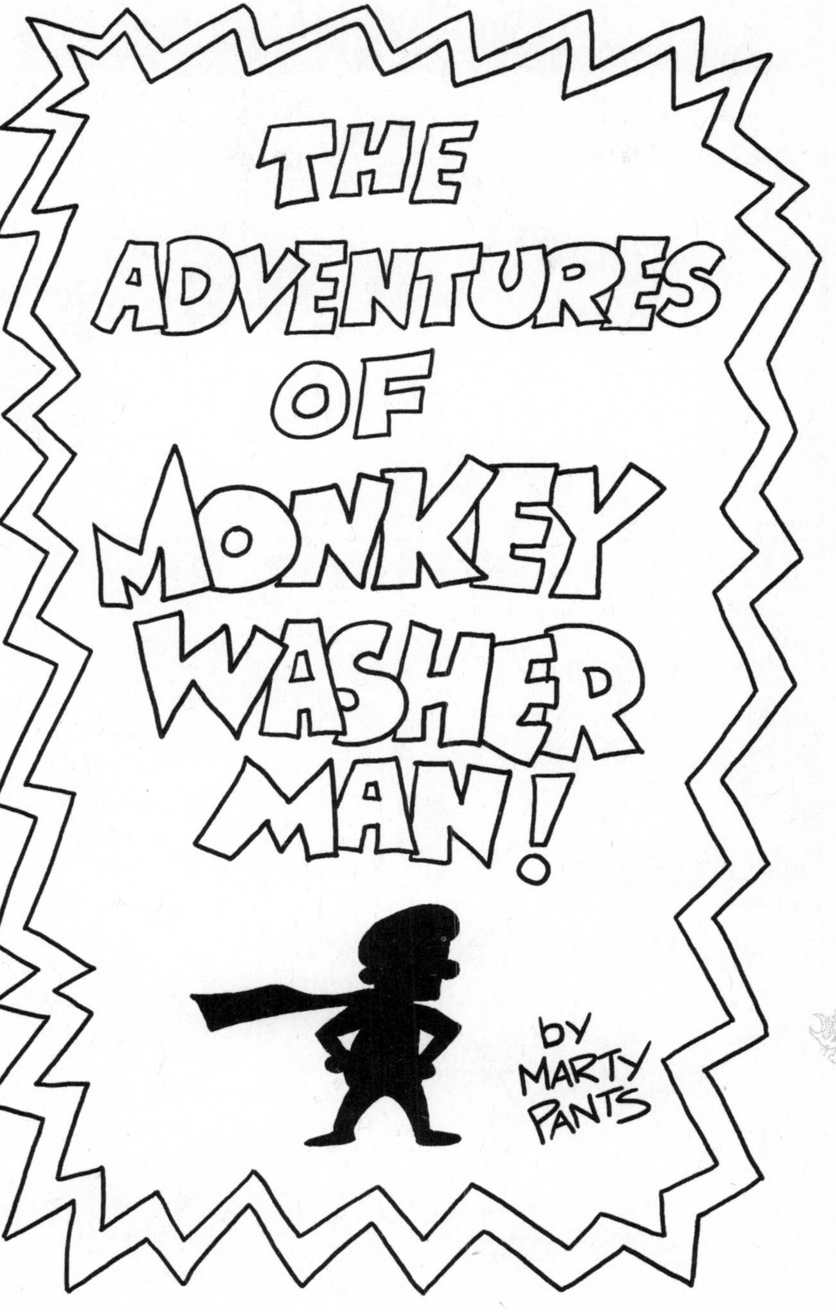
THE ADVENTURES OF MONKEY WASHER MAN!
by MARTY PANTS

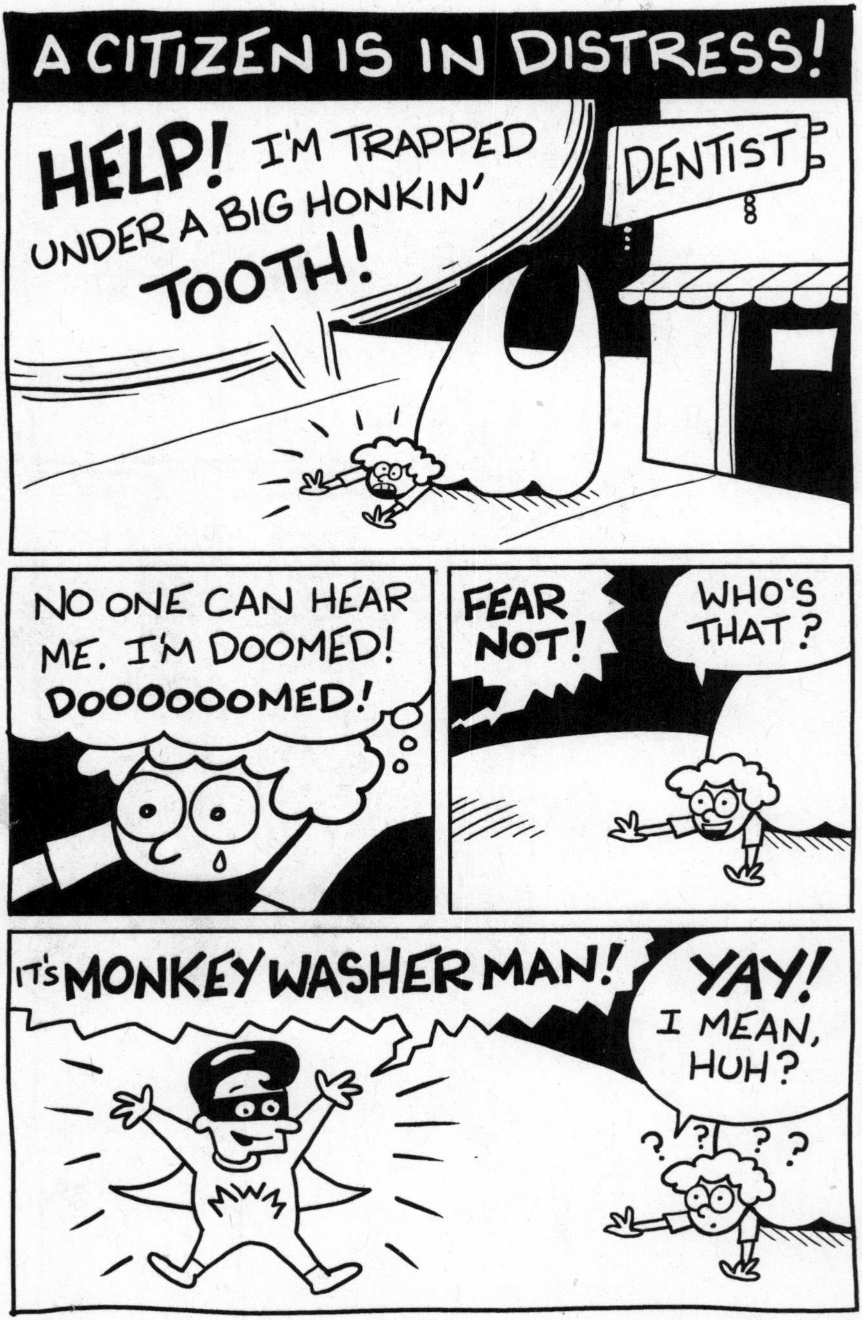
A CITIZEN IS IN DISTRESS!
HELP! I'M TRAPPED UNDER A BIG HONKIN' TOOTH!
DENTIST
NO ONE CAN HEAR ME. I'M DOOMED! DOOOOOOMED!
FEAR NOT!
WHO'S THAT?
IT'S MONKEY WASHER MAN!
YAY! I MEAN, HUH?
? ? ? ?
MWM

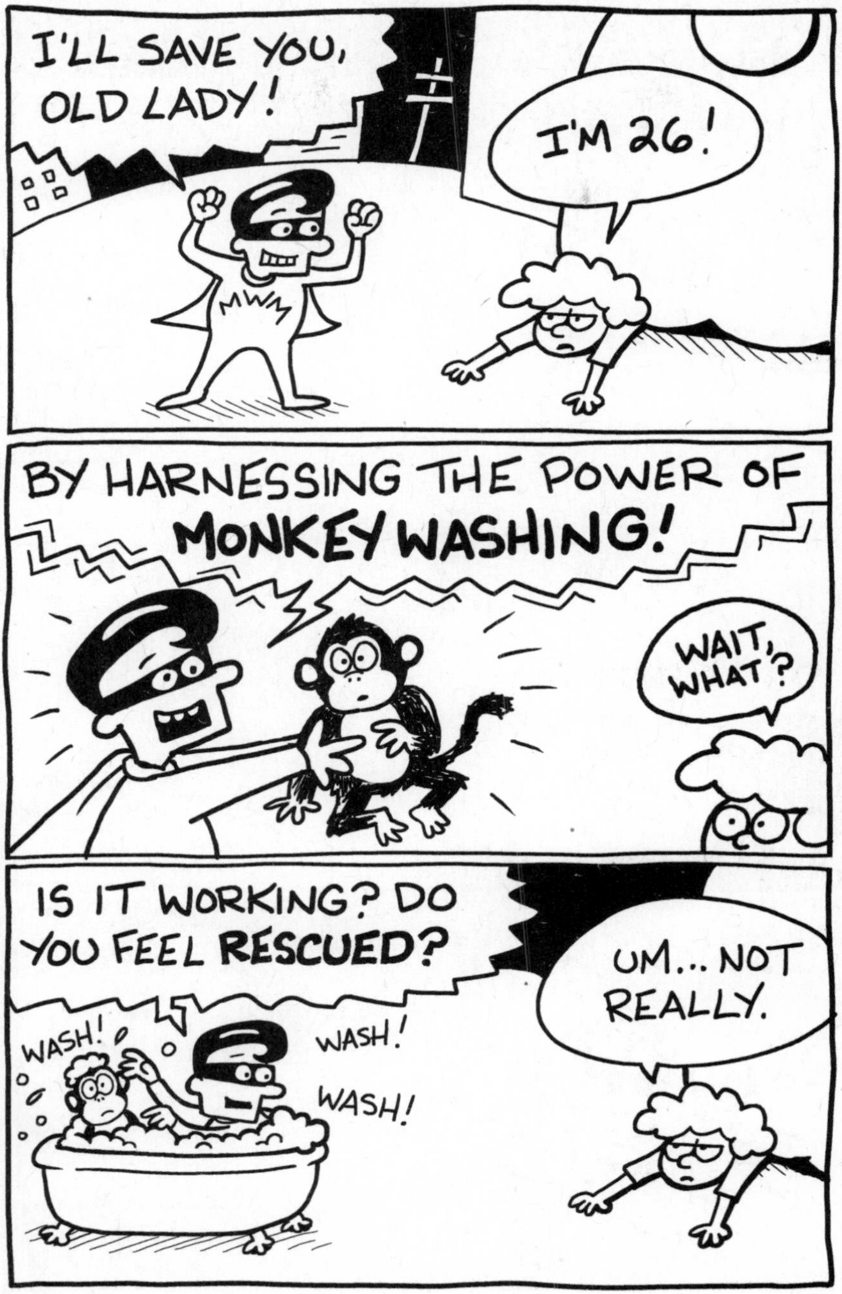
I'LL SAVE YOU, OLD LADY!
I'M 26!
MWM
BY HARNESSING THE POWER OF MONKEY WASHING!
WAIT, WHAT?
IS IT WORKING? DO YOU FEEL RESCUED?
UM... NOT REALLY.
WASH!
WASH!
WASH!

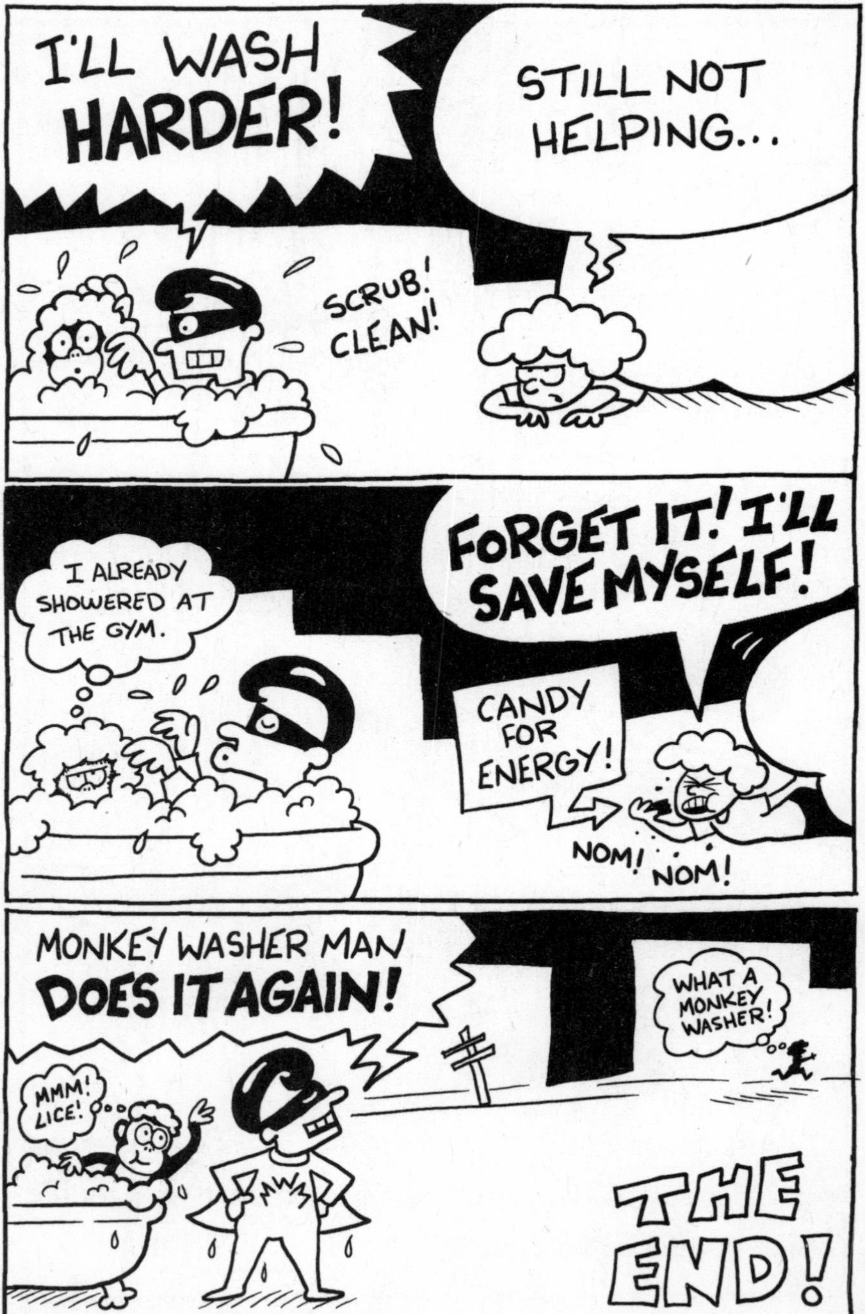
I'LL WASH HARDER!
STILL NOT HELPING...
SCRUB! CLEAN!
I ALREADY SHOWERED AT THE GYM.
FORGET IT! I'LL SAVE MYSELF!
CANDY FOR ENERGY!
NOM! NOM!
MONKEY WASHER MAN DOES IT AGAIN!
WHAT A MONKEY WASHER!
MMM! LICE!
MW
THE END!

This should be on TV!
Let's see what my best friend thinks of it.

NOM NOM

Jerome thinks it's delicious.

I just have to make sure Principal Cricklewood never sees Monkey Washer Man, or I'll get in deep trouble. Make that DEEPER trouble.

I hide it in an envelope.

I tuck the drawings into my backpack for safekeeping.

Okay, Marty, no more procrastinating. It's time to write that apology.

Really this time.

But now I'm too tired. And Jerome wants his belly rubbed.

I'll write it tomorrow morning.

I'm sure I'll remember.

CHAPTER 4

mmmm

I wake up and feel like I'm forgetting something. But then I smell

BACON!

My mom always makes an awesome breakfast before she leaves on a business trip.

I rush downstairs, and pretty soon it sounds like we're a family acappella group.

Everything is right with the world, until my mom ruins the mood.

"Did you two finish your homework?" What a buzzkill.

Erica is such a show-off!

"What about you, Marty?" my mom asks.

"Mmmm," I say, and hope there's no follow-up question. Truth is, I forgot.

I knew I forgot something! That must be what it was! My homework. I'll do it on the way to school.

Once the table is clear, Erica starts doing EVEN MORE homework. She can't stop showing off!

I ask her what she's working on but she won't tell me.

She's probably inventing a new way to annoy me.

As my dad does the dishes, he pulls some bacon from his pocket.

Smart. I wish I had saved my bacon. I gave most of mine to Jerome. Not sure why. Must be those eyes.

"So, Marty," my mom asks as she wheels her suitcase to the door. "Are you and Simon getting along?"

"Best buds," I lie.

"Good. I don't want any more calls from your principal. I can't understand what the problem is. Simon seems so *charming*."

"Mom, can I be serious for a moment?"

"I have my doubts, Marty."

"Do you believe in, um, magic?"

"I'll believe in magic," my mom says as she walks out the door, "the day your father remembers our wedding anniversary!"

That wasn't a real answer.

Maybe Erica will give me a real answer.

"Erica, do you think magic is real?"

"Do you want it to be real?" Erica asks.

"No, not really," I say.

"THEN IT'S REAL! SO REAL! THE REALEST!"

I get the feeling she's making fun of me.

My dad will definitely give me a straight answer.

"Hey, Dad. Do you believe in magic?"

What happens next is horrifying. Don't turn the page if you have a weak stomach. I warned you.

Gurk! He's singing an old song! It's beyond horrible! Someone make it STOP!

Luckily, Erica steps up.

CHAPTER 3+2×9÷9

mathzilla

I do my homework on the way to school with the help of my friend Roongrat.

"I'm glad you're a slow walker, Roonie."

"It's superior for the environment," Roongrat says. "Slow walkers burn up fewer of the planet's precious air particles. That's a scientific fact."

Roongrat makes a great work space, but his "facts" usually make no sense.

Especially when he talks about his favorite subject: Simon.

"Check it out, Marty! Simon drew a true work of art on my arm area."

I don't have to look at Roongrat's arm to know what Simon drew. Simon only draws one thing.

"Give me a break, Roonie. That's literally the only thing Simon draws!"

"It's a creative choice," Roongrat says. "Simon turns his artistic brain motions into one magical image."

Yes, having a friend who's wrong all the time can be annoying, but I've figured out how to use it to my advantage.

When I need to know something, I ask for Roongrat's opinion, then believe the opposite.

It's my system.

"Roongrat," I ask casually. "Is magic real?"

Roongrat looks into the sky.

IT'S A MYSTERY.

"Gurk! You're messing up my system, Roonie! You've got more opinions than anyone I know!"

"Correct. And my opinion is, it's unknowable, unfathomable, and undecidable."

"But . . ."

"Unbrainable, uncraniable, unpolishable . . ."

"Fine!" I say. "Be that way."

I still can't figure out if magic exists, but at least I finish my homework in time for school.

A train leaves Chicago going to Detroit traveling 50 mph. Another train leaves Detroit going to Chicago at 40 mph. Detroit is 240 miles from Chicago. How far are the trains from Chicago when they pass? Show your work.

THE TRAINS NEVER PASS

CHAPTER 6

anemone of my enemy

Roongrat heads to class, but Ms. Ortiz stops me in the hall.

HI, MARTY!

"Hi, Ms. Ortiz!"

She's the office lady and my favorite school adult. Ms. Ortiz is always on my side when things go wrong.* She must have good news for me.

* And things go wrong a lot.

"Principal Cricklewood is waiting for you in her office."
That's not good news!

Ms. Ortiz walks me to the door and says "Good luck" as she lets me in.

When I enter, I see Simon's already there. "This is for you," I hear him say as he hands Cricklewood something he drew. I'll let you guess what it is.*

"Simon!" Cricklewood gushes. "You have talent!"

"*Talent* is a strong word," I mumble.

"Good morning, Marty," Cricklewood says as she turns to me. "Did you write that apology for Simon?"

Gurk! THAT'S WHAT I FORGOT!

I'll bluff. "Of course I did!"

* I won't tell you what he drew, but it sounds exactly like AnemoneBob TrapezoidShorts.

I reach into my backpack, pull out the first thing I can grab, and say, "It's right here!"

Gurk! Of all things to grab, why did it have to be Monkey Washer Man?! Cricklewood can never see this!

"Go ahead and read it," Cricklewood says.

I stare at the envelope, clear my throat, and pretend to read.

"Dear Simon," I say in a sincere voice. "I'm very, very, very, very, very sorry that I have to apologize to you."

I think I nailed it, but something Cricklewood says makes me think she's not impressed.

Then she does the worst thing possible.

If Cricklewood looks at Monkey Washer Man, I'm dead! Out of school! I hold my breath.

"Very funny, Marty," Cricklewood says.

Then she flips it over, writes something on the other side, and hands it back. I grab the envelope and start breathing again.

"Read!" Cricklewood barks.

I peek at what she wrote, and all my happiness drains away. "Don't make me!" I plead.

"Have it your way, Marty," she says as her finger hovers over the phone.

Gurk! Fine. I grit my teeth and read.

"Dear Simon. I'm sorry I was a naughty boy and called you bad names. I was immature. You are actually very talented. Please accept my apology."

It's like poison on my tongue, but somehow I get through it without vomiting. At least it's over.

"Again, Marty," Cricklewood insists. "Louder this time."

"This is torture!" I say. "Is this legal?"

"I assure you it is."

I take a deep breath.

DEAR SIMON! I'M SORRY I WAS A NAUGHTY BOY!

When I'm done, I feel sick.

"Maybe one day," Simon says, "I can find it in my heart to forgive you."

"That's the spirit!" Cricklewood cheers.

"You're the best principal in the history of principals, Ms. Cricklewood," Simon gushes as we're scooted out the door.

"If only all youngsters were as charming as you, Simon."

Charming?

"As for you, Marty," Cricklewood adds, "consider this *Strike One*. Three strikes and you'll be suspended."

One thing's for sure. That did not go well.

CHAPTER 7

get back

I actually called Simon "talented." Time to visit my psychologist. Luckily, she's in my class.

PARKER

"I need therapy, Parker. I'm traumatized."

"You sure do," Parker says. "But maybe we should schedule it for later, Marty. Class is about to start."

She's right. I can't risk getting into trouble since I already have Strike One.

As I head to my seat, Parker reaches over and rips something off my back. "This yours, Marty?"

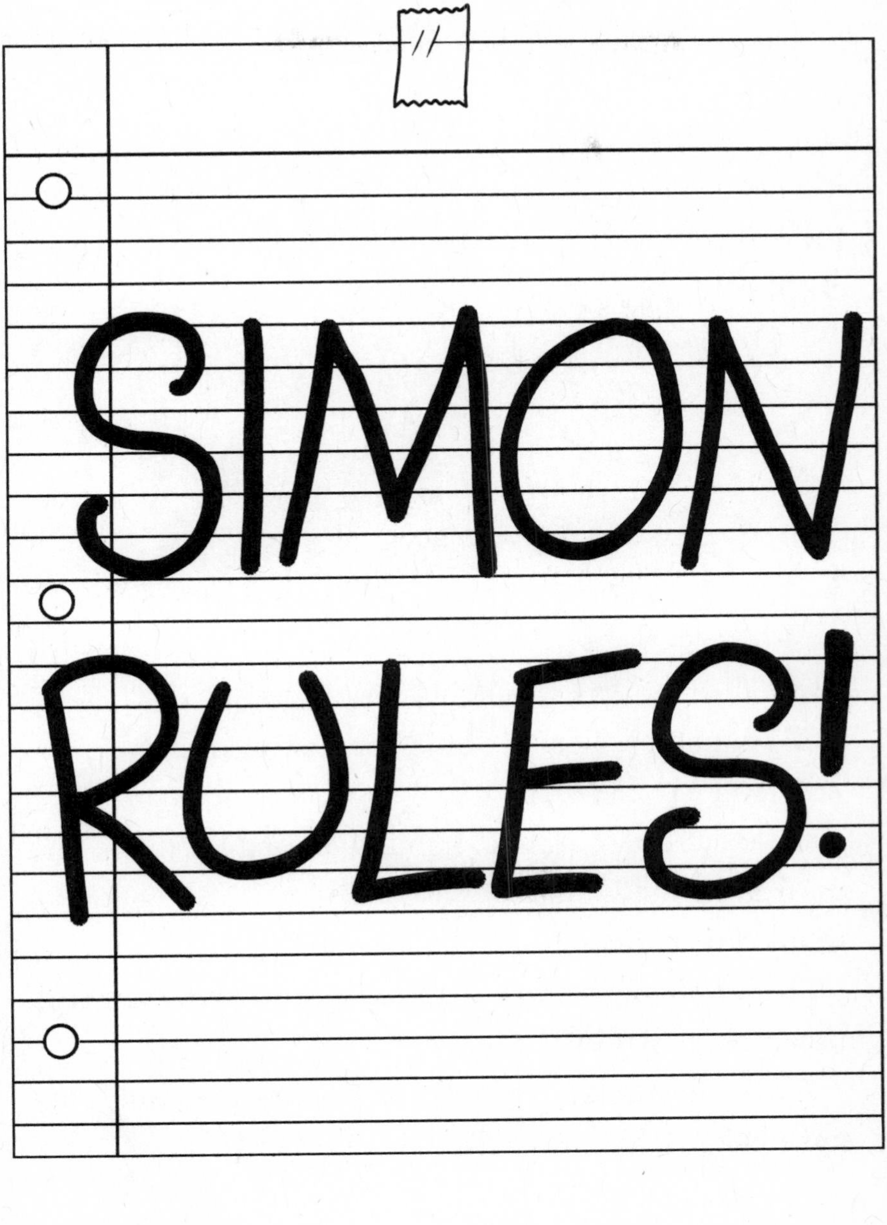
SIMON RULES!

Gurk! I grab it out of her hand. How did Simon get this on my back? Without me noticing? I'm a noticer!*

I sit down and stare at it. Then I hear my name.

MARTY, ARE YOU PASSING NOTES?

McPhee thinks I wrote this?

"What note?" I say as I hide it under my desk.

"Hand it over, Marty."

The last thing I want to hand to *anybody* is a note that says "SIMON RULES!"

I'll bluff.

"It's my dad's prescription for hemorrhoids," I say. "His face is covered with them."

"Hand it over, Marty," McPhee repeats as he holds out his hand.

* In fact, I noticed you just looked at the bottom of the page.

I don't want to give it to him, but I can't risk getting Strike Two.

I hand it over.

McPhee holds it up for everyone to see.

"'SIMON RULES!'" McPhee says, loudly. Simon starts to snicker.

"Marty, it's nice to know you think so highly of Simon," McPhee continues. "But next time you want to tell him how wonderful he is, please wait until after class."

Now the entire class is snickering. McPhee hands me back the note.

If I had magic powers, I'd make myself evaporate right now.

When I get home, Erica is working on her science project again. I can tell she's dying to tell me what it is.

NONE OF YOUR BUSINESS...

I don't care anyway. I have enough to think about.

Speaking of thinking, this is a sculpture by Auguste Rodin called *The Thinker*.

Apparently, some people like to do their thinking naked and sitting on a rock. Not me.

I prefer my beanbag of solitude.

MY BEANBAG OF SOLITUDE

It's the perfect place to unwind and think. And it's more comfortable than a rock.

So I sit and think about my problems.

And my biggest problem is Simon!

I pull that horrible "SIMON RULES!" note out of my pocket.

Jerome yanks the note out of my hand.

And he treats it the way it deserves to be treated.

Good boy!

Jerome quickly shreds the word *RULES*. He never did like rules.

As I watch my adorable cat chew up the horrible, mysterious, and inaccurate note, I can't help wondering how Simon managed to get this note on my back.

Could he actually have magic powers? Is that even possible?

I need some kind of sign.

I close my eyes and think . . .

When is the time to worry about Simon?

Then I open my eyes.

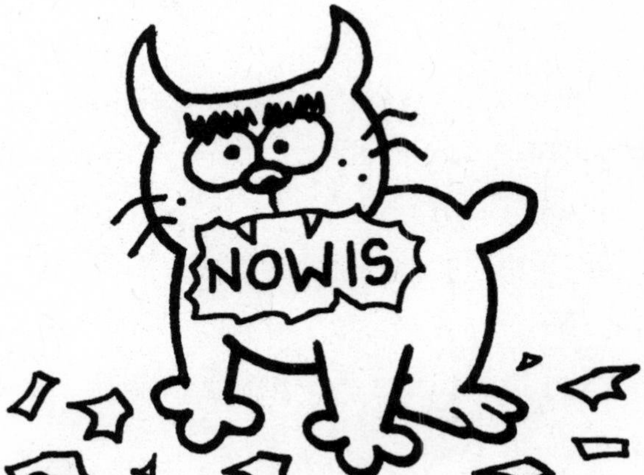
NOW IS

ostriches and ocelots

If I've learned anything in life, it's to pay attention to notes I find in Jerome's mouth.

And this one didn't say "NOWIS" a minute ago.

It said "SIMON."

How did the note change?

The only explanation I can think of is

I bet there's a hidden message in here. And I'm an expert on hidden messages. I bring the note to my dad's computer. I type the letters *N O W I S* and see what I can come up with.

Nude **O**strich **W**ith **I**tchy **S**pot

Never **O**pen **W**indows **I**n **S**pain

Noisy **O**range **W**orm **I**nterrupts **S**nake

Nasty **O**lives **W**ill **I**nfiltrate **S**alad

Napping **O**celot **W**inks **I**nvoluntarily **S**ometimes

Nothing **O**ccurs **W**hen **I** **S**leep

Nutritious **O**ctopus **W**iggles **I**nside **S**hark

Nice **O**ld **W**oman **I**s **S**melly

Hmmm. I don't think I'm on the right track. Or to put it another way:

None **O**f (these) **W**ords **I**nduce **S**atisfaction.

"Marty," my dad says as he sneaks up behind me. "I need my computer to look up some supercool song lyrics."

"But I'm doing very important homework," I tell him.

My dad looks at the screen and says, "Just what kind of homework is McPhee giving you?"

"Actually," I say, "this has to do with Simon."

"Oh, that charming friend of yours?"

"DON'T CALL HIM THAT!" I snap.

"Charming?"

"No, a friend of mine!"

Wait. I just realized what "NOWIS" stands for!

CHAPTER 10

pkzzitvftsh

I'm late for my therapy appointment! So, I jump on my bike.

BIKE ➞

You may have noticed that's not a bike. I can't seem to draw bikes. But drawing big eyeballs is fun, so I do that instead. Just go with it.

Once I arrive at my psychologist's house, I notice she's on her skateboard.

"PARKER!" I yell as I practically fall off my bike. "I have fascinating news!"

"Yay! Let's hear it!"

"Splut frmt ksht," I say.

"That does sound fascinating, Marty."

"Shrphy," I say. "It's hard to dzurphkkah when Dewey's tonguish inmee mrrfh!"

Dewey's licking my face because I ate some of his favorite food today.*

Parker wrangles Dewey, and we begin my therapy session.

"It's about Simon," I say. "He's not normal."

"Well, is anyone normal?" asks Parker.

"Maybe not, but he's EXTRA not normal."

"What do you mean?"

"I have reason to believe," I say slowly and dramatically, "that Simon is charming!"

"I suppose he can be charming," Parker says.

"I mean it literally! He's a *charmer* who is *charming* people with magic *charms*!"

* EVERY food is Dewey's favorite food.

"Fantastic!" Parker says. "Now, what would make you think ..."

"THIS!" I say as I show Parker the note.

"It used to say 'SIMON,' but it suddenly changed to 'NOWIS.'" Then I tell Parker what "NOWIS" stands for.

"You have an upside-down way of seeing things," Parker says.

"Nice of you to say," I say. "It's the only way to explain why Simon's considered the school artist even though he only draws ONE THING!"

"I bet his evil magic is the reason I can't draw bikes!" I continue. "I'm even beginning to suspect he makes me miss the toilet sometimes! He makes bad things happen, Parker."

"You miss the toilet sometimes?"

"Focus on what's important, Parker."

"Well, you occasionally use my bathroom, so . . ."

"Blame Simon. There's no other explanation."

"Classic Marty logic," Parker says.

"Thank you. I think I've proven my pkzzitvftsh . . ."

"Dewey really likes you," Parker says. "Smart puppy."

My glasses get knocked off and smudged with dog saliva. As I clean them on my shirt, I notice it's getting windy. Really windy.

I put my glasses back on.

Gurk! Dewey's slobbered me right down the hill!

In the distance, I can hear Parker cheering, "GO, MARTY! GO!"

Going is not a problem. Stopping is!

Luckily, a thoughtful citizen steps in to help me out.

I land on the soft grass. The thoughtful citizen lands on the not-so-soft sidewalk.

"Thanks for saving my bacon, citizen," I say as I brush myself off.

The citizen doesn't answer. In fact, he's not moving at all.

"Sir?" I get closer to make sure he's breathing.

He is. And his breath is terrible.

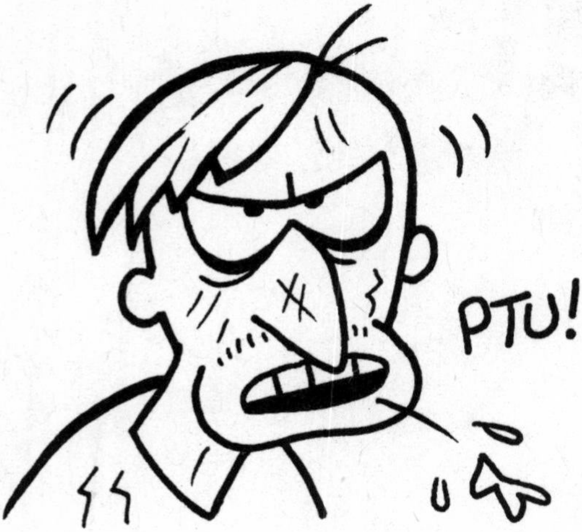
PTU!

the pits

Peach Fuzz! Why did it have to be Peach Fuzz?

PEACH FUZZ PRIMER

Real name: Salvador Ack
Identifying feature: Peach-fuzz mustache
Calls me: Wetty Pants
Occupation: Bully, punk, no-good hoodlum
Age: Undetermined
Turn-ons: Spitting, punching, spitting again
Turnoffs: Grammar, rabies shots, me

Peach Fuzz picks on me when he's in a bad mood. And he's always in a bad mood.

"Weddy Pantz!" he snarls. "Ya think nocking me ovah was funny, doo ya?"

"Kinda," I say. "I mean, NO! It was an accident!"

"Wel, I'm gonna axidentally doo this!" Peach Fuzz says as he puts me in a headlock and sets his knuckles in a familiar position.

Ow! Has anyone ever been noogied to death? I think I'm about to find out.

Yes! My dad saved my bacon!

"Gotta go, Salvador!" I say. "Let's not do this again sometime."

Peach Fuzz lets me go and whispers, "Yer safe now, Weddy, butt I'll getcha reel good next time."

Gurk. I sprint to my dad at the front door.

"Marty, are you hanging out with that no-good Salvador Ack?"

"No, I just bumped into him."

"Well, your teacher called."

"THAT'S AWESOME!" I've never been this happy about McPhee calling the house before.

"Apparently, you're still not taking your homework seriously."

"Am, too!" I say. "McPhee just doesn't understand that questions can have more than one answer."

"And your principal called."

Gurk.

"She said you're two strikes away from being suspended. What's going on? Are you tormenting Simon?"

"What? NO! That's what Simon *wants* you to think!" I explain. "He's tormenting ME. He's using magical mind control on Principal Cricklewood to make her kick me out of school! He's an evil wizard, don't you see? I bet Simon's controlling your mind right now, Dad! RIGHT NOW!"

"Marty, while I fight for control of my brain, how about you go to your room? And clean it for once."

"Fine," I say. "But I thought your brain was stronger, Dad."

"And, Marty, please don't say anything about any of this to your mother."

I march upstairs.

Simon's causing me all kinds of stress, but I'll be okay once I settle into my beanbag of solitude.

Nothing calms me down like my beanbag of solitude. I can always count on it to . . .

GURK!

CHAPTER 12

emotional baggage

"JEROME! YOU KILLED MY BEANBAG!"

He's never done anything like this before. Never.

Okay, sure, Jerome's been known to be a little aggressive with people sometimes.

Like with my dad.

And the neighbor.

And Erica.

And the vet.

And Peach Fuzz.

And McPhee.

And the animal control guy.

And my mom.

You get the idea. But he's like that with *everyone else* in the world, not me. We're compadres!

I can only think of one explanation for this.

Simon! He magically made Jerome destroy my beanbag!

Wait. Am I just blaming Simon for things he has nothing to do with? Am I jumping to conclusions? I need to be logical about this. I need logical, scientific proof.

And nothing is more logical than a flowchart.

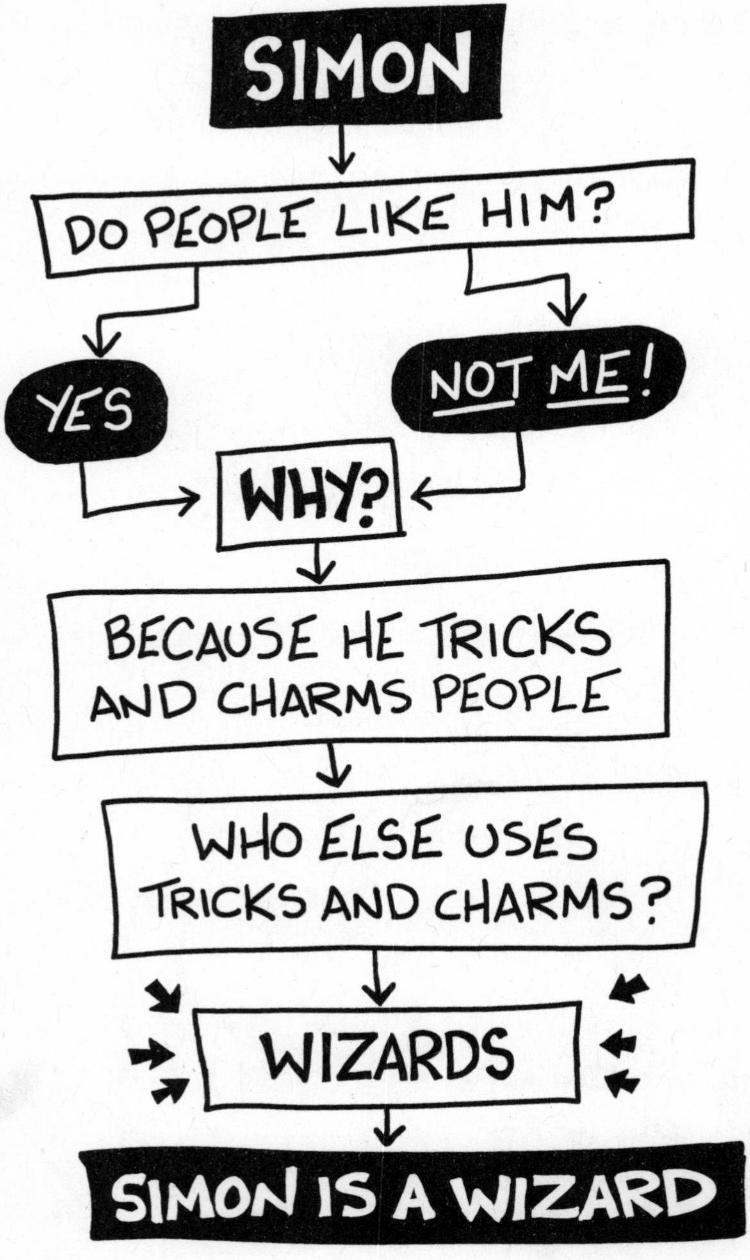
SIMON
DO PEOPLE LIKE HIM?
YES
NOT ME!
WHY?
BECAUSE HE TRICKS AND CHARMS PEOPLE
WHO ELSE USES TRICKS AND CHARMS?
WIZARDS
SIMON IS A WIZARD

That's scientific proof!

Wow! Simon is actually a wizard! I knew it!
I head to the fridge and grab a piece of bologna.

Where was I? Oh yeah. Simon! He's definitely a wizard! Now I have to figure out if he's a *good* wizard or an
evil wizard.

CHAPTER 13

that was easy

Done. Simon is an evil wizard.

How do I know?

Duh. BECAUSE HE'S SIMON!

SIMON
(artist's rendition)

And what do evil wizards always want to do?

TAKE OVER THE WORLD!

I need to stop him. But how?

I'll visit the Temple of Wizarding Knowledge.

CHAPTER 14

overbooked

"Can I help you, young man?" the librarian asks.

"I need all your books on evil-wizards-who-want-to-take-over-the-world," I say.

"I'm sorry," the librarian says. "But I can't give them to you."

"You must! The fate of the world depends on it!" I tell her.

"Someone else beat you to it," she says. "That guy over there reserved all the books on evil-wizards-who-want-to-take-over-the-world."

Just my luck!

I guess I'd rather not read that many books anyway. Looks like a lot of hard work.

What I need is an easier way to learn about stopping evil wizards.*

* Easier ways are my favorite ways.

what a card

My sister's door is partially open. I'm sure that means it's okay to bother her.

"Erica..."

"You read a lot of books, right?"

"More than you, that's for sure. Now, GO AWAY."

"So, you must have learned about ways to defeat evil wizards."

"Whatever. Now, GO AWAY."

"Could you share your knowledge with me? It's important."

"If I tell you, will you GO AWAY?"

"I promise," I promise.

"A wizard is usually defeated by a stronger wizard," Erica says. "Now, GO AWAY."

Of course!

It takes a wizard to defeat a wizard! That's called fighting fire with fire!

Although, that analogy never made much sense to me.

But where can I find a stronger wizard?

Could I be a wizard? Is it possible?

Am I like Harry Potter and Simon is like Voldemort? It's just as logical as everything else in my head.

I need to find out.

"Dad, can you turn down that terrible old music and come over here?"

"It's great music, Marty. If you listen to the lyrics . . ."

"DAD!"

"Fine. You have my attention. What's up, Marty?"

My dad picks a card from the deck and doesn't show it to me.

"Dad, your card is the four of hearts!" I declare.

"Queen of clubs, Marty."

That settles it. I'm not a wizard.

I have no choice. I have to disturb She-Who-Must-Not-Be-Disturbed.

CHAPTER 16

nugget

"Erica!" I say. "Have I ever told you you're the smartest sister I have?"

"I'm the *only* sister you have."

"Don't get bogged down in details," I tell her.

"Marty, you promised to leave me alone!"

"And I plan on keeping that promise, but first I need to know if there's another way to defeat a wizard."

"But, Erica, you're so intelligent and well read and adequate looking and . . ."

"I'M ALSO BUSY! LEAVE ME ALONE!"

"Pleeeeeeeeeeeeeeeeeeeeease?"

Erica picks up a pen. It looks like she's going to throw it at me, but instead she starts writing.

"HERE!" Erica yells as she rips the page out of her notebook and thrusts it at me.

HOW TO DEFEAT A WIZARD!

1. Dress in white
2. Cover yourself in mud
3. Hop on one foot
4. Stuff toilet paper in your ears
5. Stick a finger up your nose
6. Sing an ancient song

"Dress in white?" I say. "But I'm an artist. I always wear black."

"And make sure there are lots of people around to laugh at you," Erica says.

I see what's going on here. My sister's making fun of me. Again.

"Now, LEAVE ME ALONE, MARTY!"

Fine.

I head to the fridge and grab all the leftover chicken nuggets. They are Erica's favorite.

CHAPTER 17

flip it good

Why is this chapter upside down?
I blame SIMON!

CHAPTER 18

musta got lost

The painter Georgia O'Keeffe was inspired by flowers.

The artist Frida Kahlo was inspired by monkeys.

The Simpsons' cartoonist Matt Groening was inspired by a spork.

That's what I need. Inspiration. I need to figure out a way to stop Simon before he takes over the world.

Instead of waiting for inspiration to come to me, I go out looking for it.

I look at clouds, cars, birds, signs, and dogs peeing on fire hydrants, but nothing inspires me.

Then I notice something. I notice that I don't know where I am. I guess I wasn't paying attention to where I was going.

I've never been in this part of town before.

A magic shop! That looks like the perfect place to get antiwizard advice! I lock up my bike and walk inside. No one seems to be around. I notice a curtain and peek behind it.

"I hope so," I say when I catch my breath. "I need advice because there's an evil wizard around here who wants to take over the world."

"What did you just say, young man?"

"I said . . ."

"I heard you the first time! WHO TOLD YOU THERE WAS AN EVIL WIZARD?!"

"No one had to tell me," I explain. "I'm good at noticing."

"IS THAT SO?" the man says.

"Yes, I'm a noticer."

"WELL, LITTLE BOY, IT SEEMS YOU NOTICED TOO MUCH!"

PREPARE TO BE...

"I noticed too much about Simon?" I ask.

"Simon?" the man asks. "Who the devil is Simon?"

"Simon's the kid at my school who's the evil wizard I was telling you about."

"OH! You think some young man at your school is the dangerous, evil wizard?"

"Of course," I say. "Who else did you think I was talking about?"

"Um, no one. No one at all," the man says. "So, what are you doing here, little boy?"

"I need advice on how to defeat a wizard," I explain.

"My only advice, little boy, is to get used to the fact that the world is about to be taken over by a handsome, powerful wizard overlord!"

 MUAHAHAHAHA!

"You give terrible advice," I say.

"Watch it, little boy. You don't want to provoke an evil wizard, do you?"

"YES!" I tell him. "That's exactly what I want to do! THANK YOU!"

I run outside.

That's it. I need to provoke Simon!

I'll make him so upset that he'll use his evil magic in front of people, and everyone will see what a dangerous wizard he is.

His evilness will be exposed!

All I have to do is make Simon mad.

Luckily, that's something I'm good at.

MY 5-STEP PLAN
TO PROVOKE SIMON

Step One: Talk to Ms. Ortiz and start a school club.

Step Two: Make a flyer about the club.

Step Three: Get people to join the club.

For some reason, Step Three is not going well. I'm having trouble recruiting members.

Who can I get to join?

Parker! Of course! She's a psychologist, not an artist, but she's always up for trying new things.

"Parker," I say. "I just created CACA!"

"Congratulations, I guess . . ."

"Want to be in CACA with me?"

"No one's ever asked me that before," she says.

"Because CACA didn't exist until this morning."

"I'm pretty sure it did, Marty."

"Let's both be in CACA together. It'll be fun."

"I'm not convinced."

"Try it and see how it feels," I tell her.

"Do you need another therapy session, Marty?"

"Maybe later. Right now, I want my CACA to be popular."

I show Parker the flyer, and she finally agrees to join CACA. So does Roongrat.

Step Four: Provoke Simon!

Simon seems happy to hear this at first, until he reads the flyer.

"I'm the school artist!" he says angrily. "You can't keep me out of an art club!"

"I just did," I say. "I'm the CACA president, and it's clear you don't meet the strict requirements to be a member."

OFFICIAL CLUB RULES

1. YOU CAN'T BE SIMON.
2. DON'T BE SIMON.
3. SIMON YOU CANNOT BE.
4. YOU CAN BE ANYONE BUT SIMON.

Simon storms off. He's steaming that he can't be in CACA.

Everything's going according to plan! Simon is really upset. Soon his anger will make him use his dangerous wizarding powers. Everyone will see!

At the first official CACA meeting, I sit and wait.

As I predicted, Simon shows up. But he's not alone.

"Marty," Cricklewood says. "You can't prevent Simon from joining a school club."

"This CACA is mine!" I tell her.

"What? Never mind. School rules. Simon's in the club. And be careful, Marty. You already have Strike One."

Cricklewood leaves.

Before I know what's happening, Simon sits at the table and says, "As an official member, I call for a new election for club president!"

"What?" I say.

"I hereby second the motion!" Roongrat chimes in.

"Wait," I say.

"Time to vote!" Simon announces. "Who wants stupid Marty to remain the club president?"

Fine. Let's vote.

"And now," Simon says, "who wants wonderful ME to be club president?"

It's a tie! Now what?

Simon snaps his fingers and says, "Let's all welcome our newest member, Carlos!"

"Three votes for me, two votes for Marty. I WIN!" Simon proclaims. "And as your new and fairly elected president, I hereby change my official title from president to KING!"

I jump up. "There! You all saw it!" I say. "Simon just used black magic to take my club away! You all saw it!"

"Sore loser," Simon says.

"Don't you see?!" I say to everyone. "He takes over CACA today. Tomorrow, THE WORLD!"

Everyone just stares at me.

Then the door bursts open.

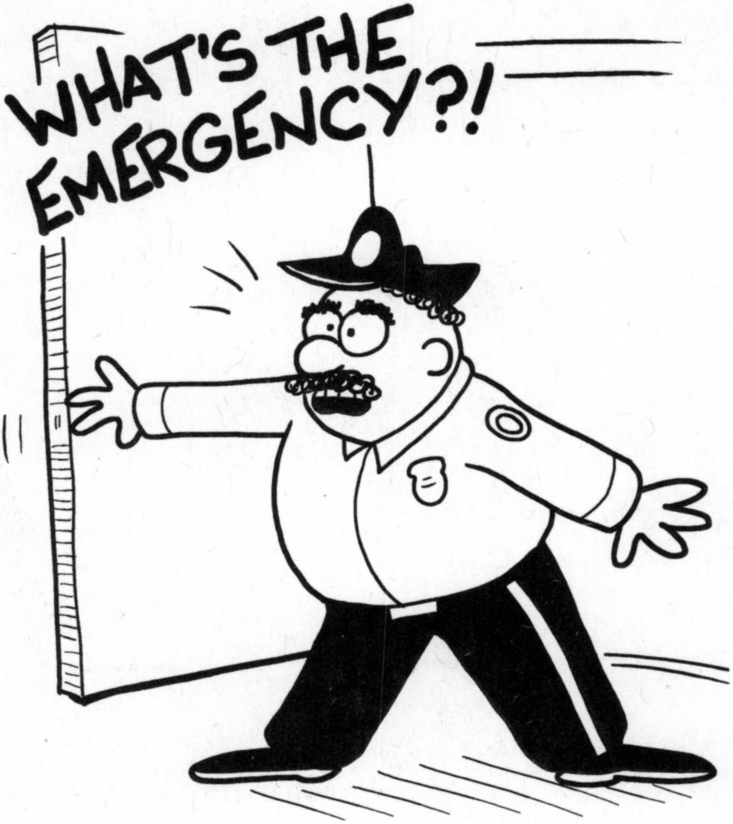
WHAT'S THE EMERGENCY?!

CHAPTER 20

things go sour

"Thank you for coming so quickly, Officer Pickels!" I say as I run over to greet him. "Simon just magically took my CACA from me! Take him away!"

I called Officer Pickels earlier so he would arrest Simon for illegal use of magic. That was Step Five of my plan. Did I forget to mention Step Five?

Step Five: Call the authorities.

But Officer Pickels doesn't arrest Simon.

Instead, he gives me a lecture.

"I like you, Marty," Officer Pickels says. "But I don't understand you sometimes. You can't call me just because you're not getting along with your friend. I thought this was a real emergency."

I want to say, "It *is* a real emergency!" and "Don't call him my friend!" But I can tell it won't get me anywhere.

Officer Pickels is a nice guy, but he's like everyone else. He doesn't notice the things I notice.

Nobody ever seems to believe me about these things, no matter how many times I'm right.

To make things worse, Principal Cricklewood pops back into the room.

One more strike and I'm suspended! Simon's getting me into so much trouble.

On the way home I realize that's been his plan all along. Turn everyone against me.

Let's hope he's not as powerful as I think he is.

At least I know there's one thing his powers could *never* do.

MAKE ME LIKE HIM.

If he ever manages to do *that*, his magic can do ANY-THING.

CHAPTER 21

the wap heard round the world

"Class, can anyone remind me where we left off?"

Weird. It's not like McPhee to forget things, but I'm certainly not about to remind him.

I mean, this could turn out GREAT! Just imagine!

All everyone has to do is keep quiet.

Gurk! Simon's going to ruin everything!

"Yes, Simon?" McPhee says.

Simon clears his throat. "You were planning to take us on a field trip to The Candy Factory!"

Holy gurk! I can't believe Simon said that! The classroom erupts.

McPhee doesn't tolerate things like this. Simon's getting detention for sure!

I bet the *whole class* gets detention.

Except me.

McPhee narrows his tortoise-like eyes and stares around the room. The class gets stone quiet.*

Here it comes.

"LISTEN UP," McPhee says. "If everyone does well on the next assignment, we can all take a field trip to The Candy Factory."

WHAT? I wait for McPhee to say he's kidding, but he never does.

* Stones have a reputation for being quiet.

WOW! A TOUR OF THE CANDY FACTORY! THIS IS AWESOME! SIMON RULES!

CHAPTER 22

hand-eye consternation

I stare at my hand through class.

I stare at my hand all through lunch.

All the way home.

All through soccer.

All through dinner.

All night.

All through my shower.

All the way back to school.

I can't believe it. I high-fived Simon!

He actually made me *like* him. He achieved the *impossible*!

Simon's magic is stronger and more dangerous than I ever imagined!

CHAPTER 23

hat trick

HOWDY, CLASS...

McPhee's in a good mood two days in a row? Impossible!

"Remember," McPhee says. "Do well on this assignment and we'll take a field trip to The Candy Factory."

Gurk. I'm trying *so hard* not to like Simon right now!

"You'll be working in pairs," McPhee continues.

Pairs? I better act fast so I can get a partner I want. My first option: Parker. I try to catch her eye, but she's already with Jasmine.

My second option: Roongrat. I look over and he's casually trying to get Simon's attention.

"Today we're trying something new," McPhee says. "You'll be pulling your partner's name out of a hat."

Something new? Since when does McPhee want to try new things?

Roongrat reaches into the hat first. I know he wants to pick Simon's name, but he seems satisfied with his pick of Jasmine.

Nikki goes next and picks Carlos.

Jen picks herself and has to try again. Monty.

My turn. And Parker is still available!

I put my hand in the hat and feel around. I touch each piece of paper. Which one feels like it has Parker's name on it?

I pick one.

Gurk! No Ordinary Wizard Is Simon!

Simon moans and pretends he doesn't want to be partners with me, but I know the truth.

He made this happen! He wants to get close to me so he can magically steal my artistic skills!

DRAMATIZATION

CHAPTER 24

foiled again

This will be the first time I've been inside Simon's house. I'm nervous. His powers must be extra strong in there.

I need to protect my brain. "Dad, is there any tinfoil?"

"I don't think they make tinfoil anymore. We have aluminum foil. Erica's using it."

It's probably not as good, but it will have to do. While my sister works on her mysterious project, I work on my own.

When I'm done, it's off to Simon's. I'm as ready as I'll ever be.

"*Friend* is a strong word," Simon says.

"It sure is!" Ms. Cardigan chirps. "Have fun, you two!"

"Really, Marty?" Simon says. "A tinfoil hat?"

"Aluminum foil," I correct him. "It's stylish. What country should we choose for our project?"

Simon says Hungary.

No, wait. He said he's hungry.

And just like magic, this happens!

Amazing! Food just shows up! Things would have gone very differently at my house.

Simon and I pig out on all the snacks while we work on our project. Then Simon's dad bursts into the room. He's coach of our soccer team.

"Hey, Marty!" he says.

"Hey, Coach."

"Stylish hat you got there, Marty!"

"Thanks, Coach."

"Now, make sure you pull your weight on this project, Marty-man! Don't drag down Simon's GPA!"

"Yes, Coach."

"My son's going to SHAKE UP THE WORLD! Simon's going to be a brilliant engineer, a star athlete, a great artist, a brave astronaut, or even president!"

"Maybe not a great artist," I mumble.

"There's no stopping my boy! YOU'LL SHAKE UP THE WORLD!"

"Yes, Dad."

"More enthusiasm, please, Simon!"

"YES, DAD! I'LL SHAKE UP THE WORLD!"

"THAT'S MY BOY!"

"Let me see what you've got so far," Mr. Cardigan says as he nudges Simon out of his seat. He looks over our project.

"NO, NO, NO!" Mr. Cardigan shouts. "This report is all WRONG!"

Before we know it, Simon's dad is doing the assignment for us!

Amazing!

First Simon uses his magic powers to get his mom to bring us snacks, then to make his dad do our homework! Wow!

We just hang out and play video games.

I have to admit Simon's wizardry is pretty *awesome*! This is the life!

Gurk! I'm starting to like Simon again. Having . . . too . . . much . . . fun . . . must . . . break . . . spell . . .

I decide to do something **bold**.

"Top of the stairs," Simon says. "Don't miss."

Just to be clear, going to the bathroom isn't the **bold** thing I'm about to do. I don't even need to use the bathroom. Well, the more I think about it, the more I actually do. But my real plan is to snoop.

I walk casually upstairs. This is what sneakers are made for. Sneaking.

Instead of heading to the bathroom, I duck into Simon's bedroom. How do I know it's Simon's bedroom?

Just a guess.

I open the closet and dig around. There's a box of old photos. I flip through and come across an old picture of Simon.

He's wearing a wizard hat!

In another, he's making something levitate with a magic wand!

I have to show these to someone! I'll show them to Officer Pickels and then he'll . . .

boom boom

Gurk. Simon's little sister Norca caught me snooping. I drop the photos and stand up.

"I thought this was the bathroom!" I say, thinking fast.

"Uh-oh!" Norca says. "You went boom boom in there?"

"No!" I say. "Thank you for stopping me just in time, Norca."

"Welcome, Marty!"

I swoop out of Simon's room and into the bathroom.

That was close. Simon must have sent her to spy on me. I guess now that I'm here I'll snoop around in the bathroom.

There's that word again! Sort of. Maybe this is the stuff that gives Simon his charming powers. I'll get rid of it all, just in case.

When I'm done, I open the door and Norca is still waiting for me. "Your hat is funny," she says.

"The word you're looking for is *stylish*," I say.

That's when I notice her doll looks just like Principal Cricklewood!

Is this how Simon controls Cricklewood? With a voodoo doll?

If I understand voodoo correctly, all I have to do is change the doll's appearance so it doesn't look like Cricklewood. Then Simon won't have any control over her anymore. I take out my marker.

There. Now Simon can't control Cricklewood unless she grows a mustache.

I head back downstairs and Norca follows.

She goes straight to her mother to tell her something. Gurk. I hope she doesn't mention my snooping.

MARTY DIDN'T GO BOOM BOOM IN THE CLOSET!

"That's nice," Ms. Cardigan says. "Play with your sister, Simon."

Whew.

The three of us play Norca's favorite video game.

We let her win.

"What are you DOING, Simon?" Mr. Cardigan barks. "Never lose on purpose! Try your hardest at all times!"

"But, Dad . . ."

"Give me the controller! I'll show you how it's done! The eye of the leopard! The horn of the unicorn! The beak of the seagull!"

Simon's dad plays as hard as he can. Shows no mercy.

He loses to a four-year-old.

I'm having a blast with Simon. I don't want to go home.

"Honey!" Ms. Cardigan calls to her husband. "Get up here! The toilet is overflowing all over the place!"

You know what? Maybe it's time for me to leave after all.

i said, good day

Simon and I get our grade on the assignment.

A+ Terrific Teamwork!

That does it. My opinion of Simon has completely changed. As far as I'm concerned, Simon is AWESOME.

He might even be my new best friend.

"Congratulations," McPhee says to the class. "Everyone did well on the assignment, so we're all going to The Candy Factory tomorrow. Everyone take a permission slip."

This is really happening! Thanks to Simon!

"A+! Wow!" my mom says at dinner. "Nice job turning things around at school, Marty!" She has another business trip and made a lobster dinner.

"I have an excellent brain," I explain.

"Of course you do," my mom says. "And how's that science project coming along, Erica?"

"Don't worry, Erica," I assure her. "You'll get used to being the second-smartest kid in the house."

After dinner, my mom kisses me goodbye and signs my permission slip.

To celebrate how wonderful things are, I give Jerome some lobster dipped in butter and catnip.

Tomorrow will be the best day in the history of field trips. I feel like my whole life has been leading up to this. I can barely sleep.

They say the great artist Leonardo da Vinci slept for only fifteen minutes every four hours.

That's what it feels like for me right now!

CHAPTER 27

field tripping

It's here! Candy Factory Day!

When we get to class, McPhee says, "We're using the buddy system for today's field trip."

"Are we pulling names from a hat?" Simon asks.

"No, I, um, gave the hat away," says McPhee. "Everyone just pick a partner."

Both Roongrat and I casually try to get Simon's attention.

But Simon pairs up with Carlos. Lucky Carlos!

Roongrat and I end up together, as usual.

That's cool. Everything is awesome today!

"Time to pass in your permission slips," McPhee says.

I reach into my backpack.

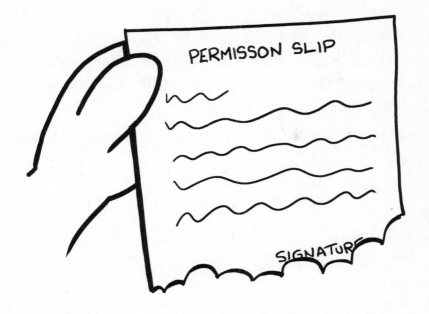

Gurk! My mom's signature is missing! Nooo!
Of course, I know where it must be right now.

I need to think quick. I'll have to bluff.

I take out a pen and forge my mom's signature on what's left of the permission slip. I hope McPhee doesn't look too closely, but he probably doesn't even know what my mom's signature looks like.

I hand it in and line up at the door with Roongrat. This is going to work!

"Marty, can you come over here?"

Gurk!

I walk to McPhee's desk. "Is there a problem, sir?"

"Marty, you expect me to believe this is your mom's signature?"

Marty's Mom

"I stand by it," I say.

"Go to the office, Marty," McPhee says. "Everyone else, follow me to the bus."

"But . . ."

"Marty. Office. Now."

NO! This can't be!

The class heads to the bus while I take that long walk to the office. I feel like I'm moving in slow motion.

All the happy voices of my classmates get cut off as the office door closes behind me.

CHAPTER 28

no nougat for you

"Hi, Marty," Ms. Ortiz says. "Mr. McPhee sent me a message informing me of the situation. Make yourself comfortable."

This. Can't. Be. Happening.

I have to sit in the office all day while everyone else goes to The Candy Factory?

CHOCOLATE

I'm going to miss the best trip in the world on a technicality?

Ms. Ortiz is usually helpful, but she's working on her computer like I'm not even there. Like this doesn't even matter!

There's laughing outside. I peek out the window and see my class boarding the bus.

I notice Principal Cricklewood is going, too! I can't handle this!

It's taking all of my concentration not to cry.

"Marty," Ms. Ortiz says.

"Quiet please," I sniff, "I'm concentrating."

"I just emailed your dad," she says. "He responded right away and gave you permission to go to The Candy Factory with your class. I'll print out the email, and it will act as your permission slip."

"Ms. Ortiz. I'm trying . . . WHAT? REALLY?"

"Really. Here you go, Marty. You're all set!"

"WOW! Thanks, Ms. Ortiz! You're the BEST!" I make a mad dash out of the office.

When I get outside, McPhee is waiting for me by the bus. "Hurry up, Marty!" he says.

I hand him my new permission slip. I made it!

Then Ms. Ortiz steps on the bus. She's coming, too? Awesome! Mr. McPhee seems as pleased as I am.

CHAPTER 29

theft by finding

♫ **ONE HUNDRED BARS** ♫
OF CHOCOLATE ON THE WALL...

The singing on the bus quiets down as The Candy Factory comes into view.

We file out of the bus and go in the front doors.

An important-looking guy gives us a boring talk about the history of the factory. I'm not listening. Then I hear, "Check your bags at the front desk, and let's all see how candy is made!"

When we walk out on The Candy Factory floor, the smell of chocolate is intoxicating!

I soon learn a few things.

1. The walls aren't edible.
2. We aren't allowed to swim in the vats.
3. We can't live here forever.

But none of that matters! This is where it all happens.

It's like floating through a dream. For once, my life feels perfect.

They even give us free candy at the end!

I think they're rejects, but who cares? They taste the same.

We all pig out, and I notice Cricklewood has a chocolate mustache.

When the receptionist hands me my backpack, it slips right out of my hand. I watch helplessly as something falls out.

Gurk!

Before I can grab my incriminating drawings, Cricklewood turns around and scoops them up.

Oh no. This is not going well.

She looks them over, and her face gets angrier and angrier.

"WHO DREW THIS?" Cricklewood snaps as she holds up the pages. Of course, she knows it was me. My signature is right on there!

This is Strike Three for sure. I'm suspended. There's no way out. It's . . .

Wait. Where's my signature?

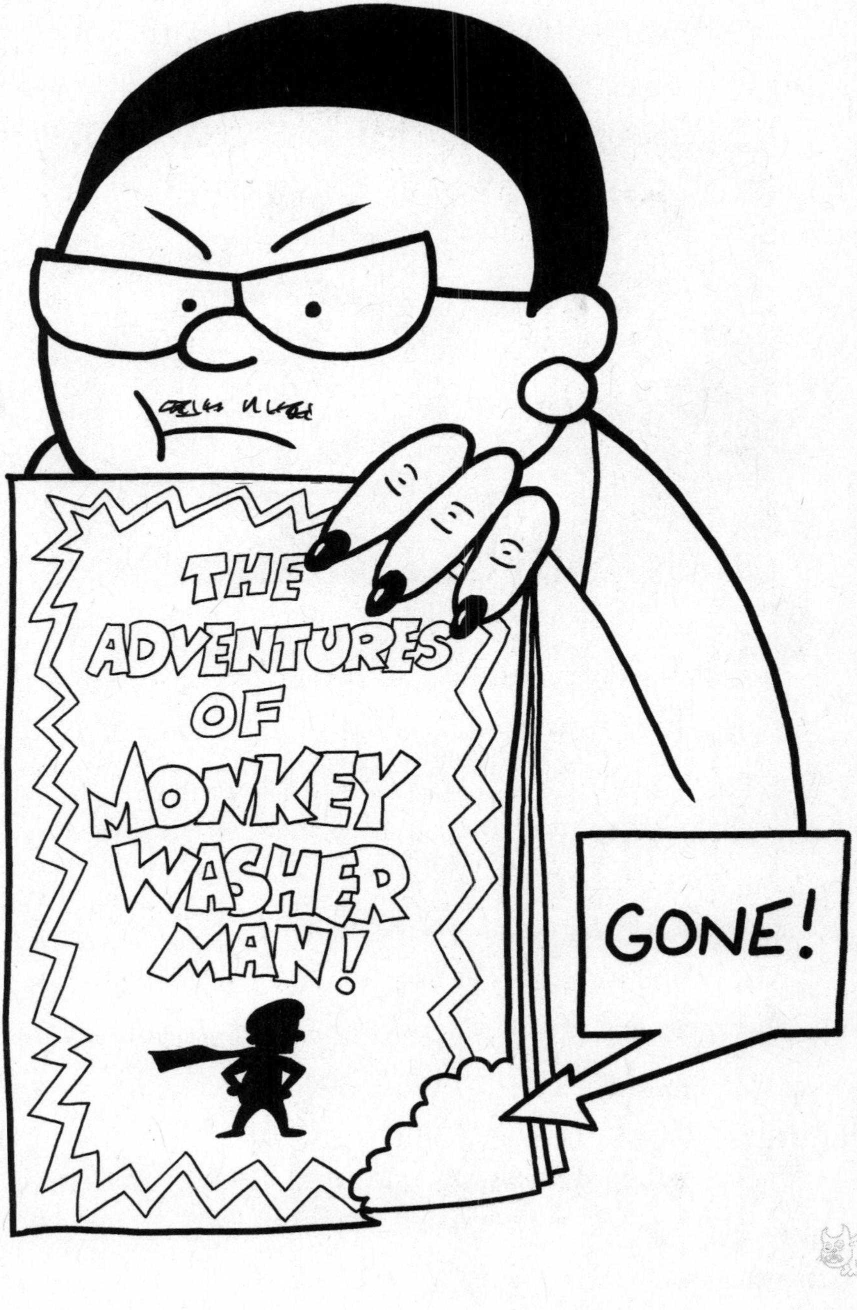
THE ADVENTURES OF MONKEY WASHER MAN!
GONE!

Of course, I know where it is.

Jerome saved my bacon!

Now there's no proof that Monkey Washer Man is mine.

"Marty, admit you drew this," Cricklewood says.

"I will not," I say.

"Marty, I know this is yours."

"Do you have proof?" I ask.

"I don't need proof," Cricklewood says. "I know it was you. You're always tormenting Simon."

"Wrong, wrong, and wrong!" I say.

"This is the LAST STRAW, Marty!" Cricklewood snaps. "I've HAD IT! This is STRIKE THREE, so you're officially suspend . . ."

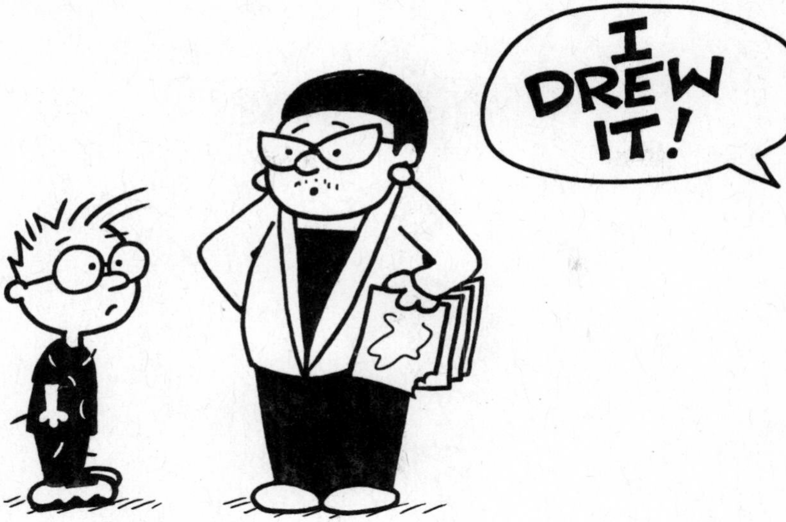
I DREW IT!

CHAPTER 30

i me me mine

"Simon?" Cricklewood asks incredulously. "YOU drew this?"

"Yup," he says. "It wasn't Marty. It was totally me."

Wow! Simon saved my bacon! That's what a best friend would do!

"That's right," I say, "Simon drew it."

The important-looking Candy Factory man looks over the drawings. He smiles and says, "This Monkey Washer thing is *fantastic*!"

"You think so?" I say.

"It's exactly the type of thing we want for our TV commercial!" he says. "You're talented, Simon!"

Wait, what? Simon is not talented. I am!

"Can we use your creative idea, Simon?" the important-looking man says. "We'll pay you."

"Of course!" Simon says. "I'll be famous!"

"Good for you, Simon!" Cricklewood says. "Your clever cartoon is going to be on TV!"

"HOLD EVERYTHING!" I calmly yell. "SIMON DIDN'T DRAW MONKEY WASHER MAN! I DID!"

Cricklewood looks at me. Something she says makes me think she doesn't believe me.

"But it's MINE!" I tell her.

"You just told me it's Simon's!" Cricklewood says impatiently.

"We all heard you with our ear holes," Roongrat says.

"I LIED!" I say, telling the truth.

"You're embarrassing yourself," Simon says.

"But . . ."

"Marty's being childish, isn't he, Ms. Cricklewood?"

"Yes, he is, Simon."

"Come on, Simon!" I plead. "Tell the truth!"

"I'm a talented, gifted artist," he says. "That's the truth."

"NO, IT ISN'T!" I snap.

"Careful, Marty," Cricklewood says.

"But it's MINE!" I say desperately. "It fell out of my backpack!" I thrust my backpack forward, and it accidentally brushes by Simon.

He falls down like he was shot by a cannon.

Then it happens.

"You're not just suspended from school, Marty," Crick-lewood shouts. "You are EXPELLED!"

yer out

"You punched Simon?!"

"I barely touched him, Dad," I explain. "Besides, it was an accident."

"And what's this about you trying to take credit for Simon's art?"

"The opposite is true! He's taking credit for MY art! With magic! You believe me, right, Dad?"

"I don't know what to believe anymore."

"Come on, Dad."

"You've been expelled, Marty! You can never go back to that school ever again! This is bad! How am I going to tell your mother?"

"None of this is my fault!" I explain. "Simon is using magic to mess with everyone's minds!"

"Does your mother know you've been obsessed with magic lately?"

"I guess so," I say. "She told me she'd believe in magic if you remembered your wedding anniversary."

"If I . . . GREAT GOOGLY MOOGLY!" my dad says. "Our wedding anniversary is THIS WEEKEND! You just saved my bacon, Marty!"

My dad runs out of my room like he's being chased by a bear.

He forgot to ground me. I know he meant to.
But he can't ground me if he can't find me.
I have to leave the house. NOW.

CHAPTER 32

another thing

"Can you believe Cricklewood expelled me?!"

"Harsh," Parker says. "Where will you go to school now?"

"I don't know," I tell her. "Probably some school for criminals.

"I'm telling you, Parker, I drew Monkey Washer Man, not Simon! You know me—that's the kind of stuff I alvw-zzz drrmllthff!"

"Blunndpsh besides," I say, "Simon couldn't have drawn it. Everyone knows he only draws ONE THING!"

ONE THING! →

"Well, Marty . . ." Parker says.

"Well, what?"

"Simon drew this for me the other day." She shows me something on her arm.

ANOTHER THING!

I recognize that. It's the famous character Hey-O Kiddie!

"Simon drew that?" I ask. "Are you sure?"

"He's been drawing it for lots of girls lately."

Wow. This is a big deal.

"Big deal!" I say. "Now there are TWO famous characters he can copy! He just sucks the talent from other people's brains, don't you see?"

"Is that what's going on, Marty?"

"Yes! But he can't suck the talent from my brain, so he just steals my drawings and convinces everyone they're his! It's black magic! He's evil!"

"The mayor is giving Simon an award," Parker tells me, "to celebrate his success with Monkey Washer Man."

"No way!"

"Yes, way. There's going to be a ceremony on Saturday. He's getting the You Little Hero award."

"They're expecting the whole city to attend," Parker continues.

"No fair! It should be ME getting that award!"

Parker looks like she wants to say something but doesn't.

"No one else believes me," I tell her. "But at least I know you're on my side, Parker."

"Marty," Parker says. "There's something I should tell you. I'm helping Simon prepare for the ceremony."

"What? WHY?"

"He asked me, and it sounded like fun. I guess I won't have much time for these psychology sessions."

I snap my fingers in front of Parker's face. "Snap out of it! You've been charmed!" I tell her.

She just looks at me.

I can't believe this.

Parker has always been the one person I could count on. The one person who understood me no matter what.

That's all over now. I can no longer trust her.

"Oh, look at the time," I say as I point to a cloud. "I have to go."

"Marty, listen . . ."

"Gxcrummmff," I say.

Not because Dewey was licking my mouth, but because I couldn't think of anything else to say.

CHAPTER 33

game over

Now, there's only one person I can turn to.

"I'm a fugitive," I tell Roongrat. "I can't go home or I'll get grounded. I don't know who to trust. Can I stay with you? I have nowhere else to go."

"Negatory," Roongrat tells me. "We're moving."

"What WHAT?"

"Due to circumstantial circumstances," Roongrat says. "My mother lost her job of employment income. Things have been monetarily difficult, and we have to stay with my aunt up north."

"Roonie!" I say. "That stinks!"

"Correctamundo." Roongrat sighs. "I attempted to help pay the rent by selling my excellent video games to Simon. It didn't result in enough moola."

Simon! Of course he's behind this.

He's slowly taking everything away from me:

My art

My beanbag of solitude

My CACA

My school

My home

My psychologist

And now my friend with the best video games.

"So, I guess I'll see you around, Roonie."

"Yes. Seeing is an important skill," Roongrat says. "And did you know certain African caterpillars can see out of their butts?"

Then I do something I've never done before, and I will not admit to it if anyone asks me.

CHAPTER 34

bush league

I don't know where to go. I have no one. I guess I'll live in the bushes in front of my house for the rest of my life.

If only someone else had seen Monkey Washer Man fall out of my backpack, then I could show everyone it was mine all along! I could expose Simon for the deceitful wizard that he is!

But there's no proof.

Wait. Maybe there is.

I noticed something at The Candy Factory.

SECURITY CAMERAS

If one of those cameras was pointed at me when Monkey Washer Man fell out of my backpack, that would prove it was mine!

I need access to The Candy Factory security footage. I close my eyes and try to think of a plan. Nothing but darkness. That's not helpful. So I open my eyes.

AAAAAAH! That's not helpful, either! I leap out of the bushes, but instead of feeling better, I feel worse.

Ouch!

"Marty!" Erica yells. "Get out of the way!"

"What was that?" I ask as I rub my head.

"I finished my science project." Erica points up in the air. "It's a drone."

"This is a legit A+," she says. "It's perfect."

"It IS perfect!" I say. Now I have my plan!

insecurity

My dad left the house to drive my sister to soccer practice. Or the movies. Or the library. Or the How to Be Difficult seminar. I take the opportunity to sneak inside.

There's Erica's drone sitting on the kitchen table. I tuck it into my backpack.

I grab a piece of paper and write down my secret plan for breaking into The Candy Factory.

Now it's time to set off on my mission.

I park my bike in the back of The Candy Factory and review my secret plan.

SECRET PLAN TO BREAK INTO THE CANDY FACTORY

1. RIDE ERICA'S DRONE UP INTO THE CANDY FACTORY VENT

2. STEAL SECURITY FOOTAGE

3. FLY OUT

Flawless!

But before I can set my secret plan into motion, I get a funny feeling. My backpack is vibrating. The drone got turned on!

Gurk! My backpack is gone, and my plan is ruined.

Now I have to try an even crazier plan. It's called Asking for Permission. I walk inside the front door and see the receptionist.

"My name is Marty Pants," I tell her. "I need to see your security videos, please. An evil wizard is stealing my ideas."

"Sorry, our security footage is private."

"It's for a school project," I tell her.

"Like I said, young man, it's private."

Wow. That "school project" line always works! She's a tough nut to crack.

Then I notice a photo on her desk, and that gives me an idea.

WORLD'S BEST GRANDMA ♥

"Well, the truth is, ma'am," I say. "I came here on a tour with my class the other day and I lost a picture of my granny. She gave it to me the day she passed away, and I look at it every day to remind me of her. We had a special bond. Never mind. You wouldn't understand the special love between a grandparent and a grandchild. I guess I'll just forget what she looked like. Sorry to bother you."

"You go right ahead, young man (*sniff*). Just don't tell anyone I let you in."

I walk through the doors. Ah, the overwhelming smell of chocolate again! Happiness! Joy!

But I can't let it distract me. I have a mission.

I notice the security cameras high up on the walls.

Then I look around at the doors and notice one with this sign.

SECURITY

I walk over and push the door. It opens.

That's not very secure.

No one's in here. Perfect. I take a seat at the monitors, but I'm not sure what to do. I press some random buttons.

TAP
TAP
TAP

There's a lot of boring video of the parking lot.

I see an empty stairway, a blank wall, a worker picking his nose, and . . . is that McPhee and Ortiz going into the custodian closet?

Wait! I see our class! That's our field trip! I somehow hit the right buttons!

And there's me! I keep watching. I look pretty dashing. Here it comes.

Yes! I see the Monkey Washer Man drawings falling out of my backpack!

There it is! Proof! Irrefutable proof that Monkey Washer Man is mine! I can finally expose Simon!

CHAPTER 36

that's just peachy

What's Peach Fuzz doing here?

"You work here?" I ask, shocked.

"Dats rite. Im da new securitee gard. Howd ya get in hear, Weddy Pantz?"

"Never mind that," I say as I point to the screen. "I need this video! It proves I created Monkey Washer Man!"

Peach Fuzz strolls over and presses a button.

"Oopz," he says. "Awl gone."

"PEACH FUZZ! WHAT DID YOU DO?!"

"Dont cawl me dat!" Peach Fuzz snaps. "NEVAH CAWL ME DAT! Tha only reeson I ain't givin' ya a beatin' rite now, Weddy, is cuz I'm workin'. Now get outta hear befour I change my mined! Let me help ya out da door!"

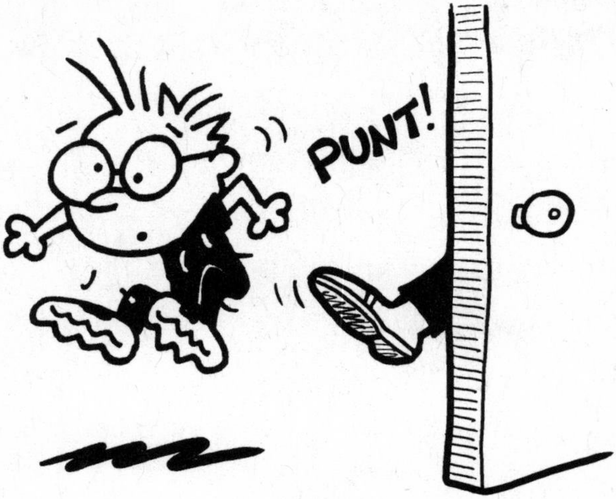
PUNT!

granny pants

Everything is going wrong! I decide to go home and accept my grounding. But instead of grounding me, my dad kicks me out of the house!

Erica and I are being forced to stay at Granny's.

It's our parents' wedding anniversary, and they're having a second honeymoon at the house. It apparently lasts more than a second, though, because they want to be alone until tomorrow.

I don't particularly like it at Granny's house. Granny and I don't really connect.

She feeds me weird things.

She says weird things.

She collects weird things.

And she prefers Erica over me. Which is extra obvious today.

"I lost my science project!" Erica whines. "It must have flown right out the window! That means a big, fat ZERO!"

Erica has never gotten anything lower than an A-.

Ever.

She's turning red, and I can't tell if she's going to scream or cry.

Granny tries to change the subject. "You know, dear, I hear you like to change the spelling of your name from time to time. My name is spelled *M-I-N-N-I-E*, but I like to spell it *M-I-N-I*. Is that cute? So, how are you spelling your name these days, dear?"

"*L-O-S-E-R*," Erica says.

"That's nice, dear. Have a candy heart. Things will be fine."

THINGS WILL NEVER BE FINE AGAIN!

Erica storms into the kitchen.

"How about you, Martin?" Granny asks. "Candy heart?" She holds out the bowl.

No one likes candy more than I do, but these look ancient.

"No, thank you, Granny Pants."

"You don't want to hurt my feelings, do you, Martin?

"Fine." I try to take one, but four more come along for the ride.

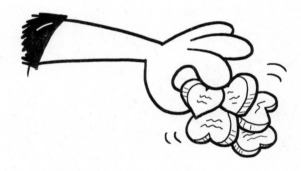

I pretend to eat them, but slip them into my pocket.

Granny shuffles into the kitchen to cheer up Erica.

Obviously, Granny doesn't care when I'm sad, only when Erica is. My life is falling apart, and all that matters is Erica.

I wonder if there's anything to eat. I walk over to the fridge, but am not sure how to open it.

Granny saved every drawing I ever gave her. Smart. They'll be worth a lot in a hundred years.

One drawing catches my eye.

Jerome. My best friend.

I need to see him. Jerome can always cheer me up, and I'm sure he misses me, too.

With Erica hogging all the attention, Granny won't even notice I'm gone.

And I'm sure my parents won't mind if I drop by the house during their second honeymoon.

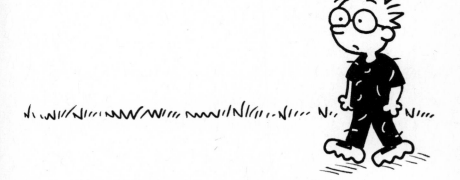

CHAPTER 38

let's do the time warp

As I approach the house, I see movement through the window. The energy feels different. I peek inside and can't understand what I'm seeing!

My dad's in a tuxedo, and my mom's in her wedding
gown. There are candles. Old, romantic music is playing.
This can only mean one thing.

I'm witnessing my parents' wedding night!

There are candles everywhere because electricity hasn't been invented yet!

How far back in time did my parents get married?

Inside my house, it's only the fifteenth century! This is crazy.

And who has the ability to send my house back in time like this? There's only one villain with that kind of power.

It's strange looking back in time. I lean on the window to get a better look.

Gurk! I have to hide! In their world, I don't exist. I haven't even been born yet! If they see me, it could mess up the past! And I've seen enough movies to know it's a bad idea to mess up the past.

"I thought you fixed the window," my mom says.

"I did," my dad replies. "I used duct tape."

"Then why is it still broken?"

"Because I didn't do a very good job?"

"Correct!"

"Can we talk about this another time?"

"We'll talk about it now," my mom says.

Oh no. My parents are fighting! And it's all my fault.

If they break up on their wedding night, then they won't have kids! I'll never be born! Erica will never be born! (I have mixed feelings about that part.)

But I definitely want to exist!

I need to get my parents back together.

If only I had a love potion.

I reach into my pocket.

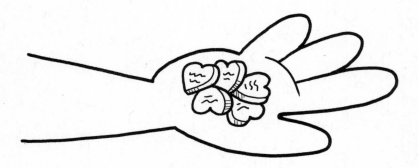

Granny's candy hearts! Maybe these will do the trick.

I toss them into the room and hope for the best.

My dad takes a sip of wine.
YES! It's working! My parents are hugging!

I better get out of here before I mess things up again!

And I didn't even get to see Jerome.

Wait.

If everything inside my house is way back in the past, what about Jerome?

- Jerome was in the house.
- My house is now way back in the past.
- Jerome didn't exist way back in the past.
- Therefore, Jerome no longer exists.

Ugh. I feel ill.

Simon finally did it. He used black magic to take away everything I care about. Even my very best friend in the whole world.

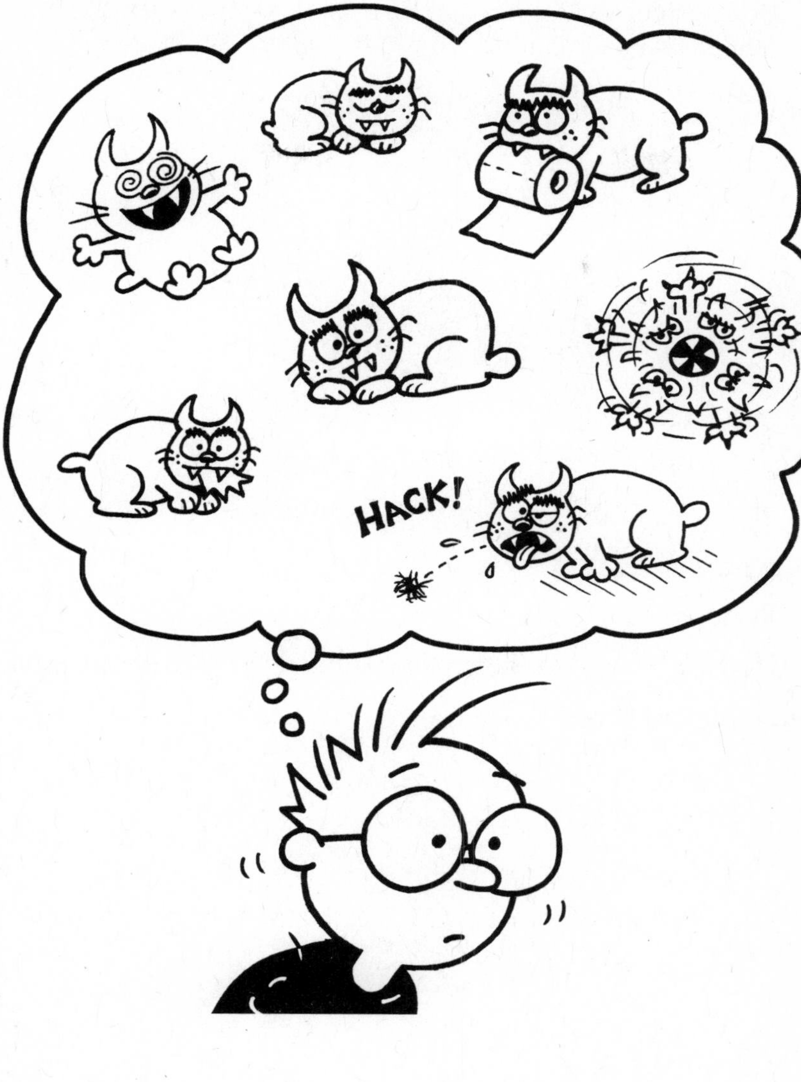
HACK!

CHAPTER 39

whack-a-doodle

When I get back to Granny's, Erica is still making a scene about losing her drone.

There are a lot more important things happening right now!

I try to show my sister that she's overreacting.

"Erica," I say, "your drone was hard to control anyway."

She looks at me.

"What. Did. You. Do. Marty?"

"Nothing." I say. "I did nothing."

"Marty, if I find out you . . ."

While Erica threatens me with all kinds of torture, I realize the world has ONE LAST HOPE. Simon has always had a big crush on Erica, but she barely notices him. That means his mind control doesn't work on her! Erica is immune to Simon's powers!

Erica must be THE ONE! THE ONE who can save the world!

THE ONE

"Erica," I say. "You don't like Simon, right?"

"Who the heck is Simon?"

"Simon is the dumb kid who's having the dumb ceremony at the stupid Candy Factory tonight. You've met him a hundred times."

"So, you want me to NOT like him?"

"Obviously," I say.

"You WHAT?"

"I ADORE him!" Erica shrieks. "I want to MARRY him. I want to have his BABY! I'm going to the ceremony tonight to PROPOSE to . . . What was his name again?"

"Simon," I remind her.

"To propose to SIMON!" she says.

My sister is going to marry Simon? Simon is going to be my *brother-in-law*?!

I didn't think things could get any worse.

But they just did.

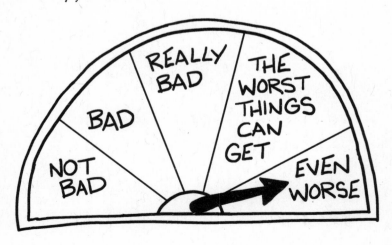

It's all too much for my brain. Tonight Simon will use his magic to take over the city. Then the ENTIRE WORLD! The wrath he will bring upon this planet is unthinkable!

And you know what I'm going to do about it?

That's right, nothing.

I'll just sit here and wait for the world to end.

"Something bothering you, Martin?"

"You wouldn't understand, Granny Pants."

"Try me."

Before I can stop myself, I blurt out, "Simon is an evil wizard who stole my art and he's also taken away everything that's important to me like my cat and family and friends and school and CACA and beanbag of solitude and tonight he's going to use magic mind manipulation on everyone and take over the city and soon conquer the entire planet until he's King of the World and then he will bring pain and misery and despair and there's absolutely nothing I can do to stop him and no one believes me anyway so I give up."

Granny Pants looks at me for a long time.

"Well, you've got to do something, Martin."

"I do?"

"Yes! We can't have an evil whack-a-doodle going around controlling feeble-brained goofballs, can we?"

"I guess not, but . . ."

"DO WHAT HAS TO BE DONE, MARTIN!"

"But I don't know what to do, Granny Pants!"

"I know you, Martin. You must have one nutzo, loony scheme left in your noggin!"

"Um, there's one ridiculous thing I could try. . . ."

"SOUNDS PERFECT!"

"Really?"

"YES! BE RIDICULOUS, MARTIN!"

"I know how to do that!" I say.

"Whatever you need, Martin. I'm here for you."

"I have a job for you." I jump up. "Do you have any aluminum foil?"

Granny opens her closet. "No, but I do have some tin-foil."

CHAPTER 40

ceremonial rhapsody

I hope I'm not too late!

I arrive at The Candy Factory and see the crowd of people taking their seats around a stage. I'm just in time! The ceremony is about to begin.

Simon's evil wizard face is being projected onto a big screen. Parker is behind the crowd working the projector.

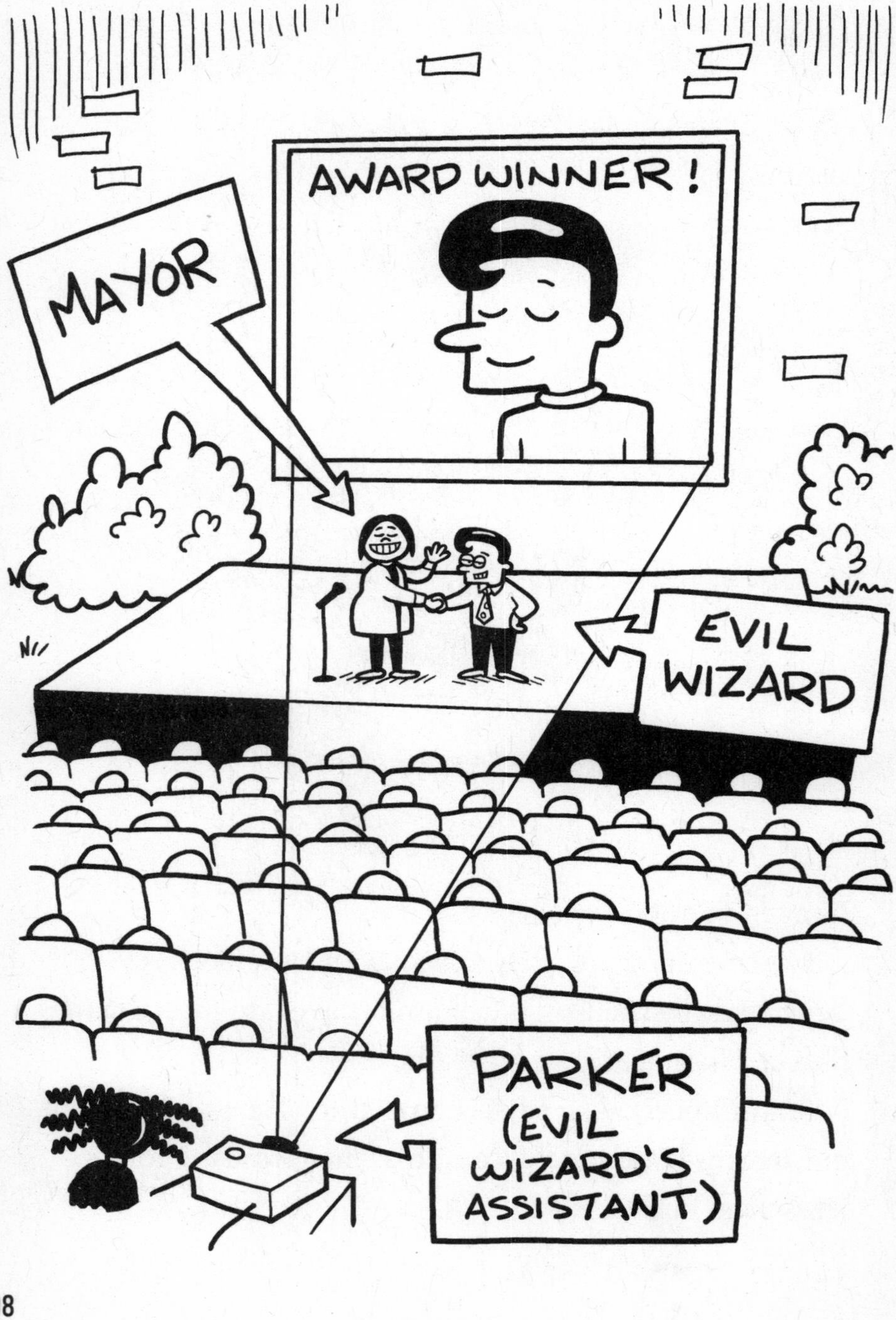
AWARD WINNER!
MAYOR
EVIL WIZARD
PARKER (EVIL WIZARD'S ASSISTANT)

Mayor Mitnic talks into the microphone.

"I am proud of this young man's artistic skills and success," the mayor says to the crowd. "He is both charming and talented. He's about to shake up the world! I'm happy to present Simon Cardigan with the You Little Hero award! Let's give him a warm Sinkhole City welcome!"

The crowd starts to cheer.

Stop clapping, everyone! He feeds off your approval!

"Thank you, thank you!" Simon says into the microphone. His voice booms over the crowd.

"I am honored to be recognized for the great artist I am, because I definitely drew this!" he says as he points to the screen behind him.

Parker presses a button on the projector and the first page of my Monkey Washer Man comic appears on the screen. IT'S HUGE!

The crowd loves it! Of course they do—it's mine and it's awesome.

Then page two comes up. The crowd is laughing as Simon reads my comic out loud. They are falling under his spell!

Wait. Why am I just standing here watching?

I have to stop him!

But something is holding me back.

"Wear do ya think yer goin', Weddy Pantz?"

"You have to let me go, Salvador!" I plead. "This is important!"

"Ho har ha!" Peach Fuzz says as he spits on the ground. "Ya ain't goin' nowear!" He squeezes my shoulder so hard, it hurts!

Then I feel a hand on my other shoulder. "Everything okay, Marty?"

It's Mr. Fedora! Parker's dad! And he brought Dewey.

"This hoodlum is mistreating me," I say.

"Dis kid cant come in!" Peach Fuzz says.

"I'll take responsibility for him," Mr. Fedora says as Dewey smells my butt.

"No wayy," Peach Fuzz says. "Im da one in charge hear and if I sazzmpthglmmftgh!"

Peach Fuzz looks terrified of Dewey. Suddenly, he doesn't seem so tough. Peach Fuzz gets up and runs away screaming, "HALP! A WILD DAWG ATE MY FACE! HALP!"

"Come on, Marty," Mr. Fedora says. "You can sit with me."

"Can you excuse me for a sec?" I ask. "I have to go into the bushes."

"Try not to be too long," Mr. Fedora tells me.

He thinks I'm going into the bushes to pee, but I don't need to pee. Well, the more I think about it, the more I actually do, but what I really need is a hiding place. I need to prepare myself for what I'm about to do.

The first bush I come across is already occupied.

So I move on to the next bush. It's occupied, too.

When I finally find a bush of my own, I hide behind it and open Granny's gigantic pocketbook. I take out her wedding dress and put it on. It fits nicely.

Then I roll around on the ground.

Now I can check off the first two things on my sister's antiwizard list.

HOW TO DEFEAT A WIZARD!

1. Dress in white ✓
2. Cover yourself in mud ✓
3. Hop on one foot
4. Stuff toilet paper in your ears
5. Stick a finger up your nose
6. Sing an ancient song

I hear the crowd applauding. The presentation is almost over! It's now or never!

I make a mad dash through the crowd, up the stairs, and onto the stage.

I grab the microphone out of Simon's hand and shout, "HEY, EVERYONE! I HAVE AN IMPORTANT ANNOUNCEMENT!"

The crowd stares at me.

"Marty, you idiot!" Simon says. "What are you DOING?!"

I ignore him and continue talking to the crowd. "SIMON CARDIGAN'S AN EVIL WIZARD! HE'S CONTROLLING YOUR MINDS! THIS CEREMONY SHOULD BE FOR ME!" Then I wait for the cheers.

The crowd hates me, but it's not their fault. They are under Simon's evil spell.

"AND NOW," I announce, "I WILL SAVE YOU!"

I complete the rest of the items on the list.

	3. Hop on one foot ✔
	4. Stuff toilet paper in your ears ✔
	5. Stick a finger up your nose ✔
	6. Sing an ancient song ✔

The ancient song I choose to sing is one I've heard my dad sing a zillion times.

SCARAMOUCHE!
SCARAMOUCHE!
WILL YOU
DO THE
FANDANGO?

The crowd watches me in stunned silence.

At least I think it's stunned silence. It's hard to tell with toilet paper in my ears.

Simon smirks, looks at the crowd, and shrugs. The crowd roars with laughter.

It's not working! I hop faster, cram my finger deeper in my nose, and sing even louder.

GALILEO!

GALILEO!

The crowd keeps laughing. They don't understand I'm trying to save them!

I look over at Parker.

Is she laughing at me, too?

It's clear I'm not defeating a wizard. All I'm doing is humiliating myself in front of the entire city, just like my sister hoped I would do.

I feel someone pull the toilet paper out of my ears.

"Come on, Marty. Let's get you out of here. . . ."

CHAPTER 41

never believe it's not so

"Marty," Officer Pickels says as he guides me offstage. "What goes on in that head of yours?"

"Righteousness," I say.

Simon waves to the crowd, and they cheer louder than ever. I only made things worse.

I put my head down. I failed to save the world. I just couldn't do it this time.

Then I hear a familiar voice.

I'm sorry to let you down, Granny Pants.

Then I hear Simon's voice, but it's not coming from Simon.

Parker turned on the projector again, and it's playing a video of Simon.

I stop to watch. Officer Pickels does, too.

"I hope you enjoyed this presentation of my awesome art!" says the Simon on the screen.

"Cut!" says Parker's voice from the video. *"We're all finished recording. You were great, Simon."*

"I know," says the Simon on the screen. *"I can be charming when I want to be."*

The crowd quietly watches the video.

"Just between you and me," Parker's voice says, *"I know Marty drew Monkey Washer Man."*

The Simon on the screen acts angry and says, *"What? That's a bunch of . . ."*

"Only a clever, handsome genius like you could get away with stealing it."

"You think?" says the Simon on the screen.

"Totally," says the Parker on the screen.

The Simon on the screen smiles and says, *"That's me, all right. I'm a handsome genius! Sure, Marty drew Monkey Washer Man, but I'll take the credit! I mean, who's going to believe HIM over ME? No one!"*

I look away from the Simon on the screen and peek over at the real Simon standing onstage.

His face is turning green.

The crowd starts to get restless. Now they're booing Simon instead of me! They're calling him a phony, a thief, a liar, and even worse words.

I glance over at the real Parker.

Officer Pickels lets go of my shoulder and whispers, "Go ahead, Marty. Do whatever you have to do. I'll look the other way."

"Thanks, Officer Pickels!"

I jump back onstage and charge right at Simon. I grab the mike.

"Told you," I say to the crowd.

DROP!

CHAPTER 42

chocolate shake

Simon is freaking out. It looks like he's going to explode.

"I'm supposed to shake up the world," he growls. "I'm supposed to shake up the world. . . ."

He closes his eyes tightly. Then he begins shaking like crazy.

Then I realize I'm shaking, too. The whole stage is shaking! Even The Candy Factory is shaking!

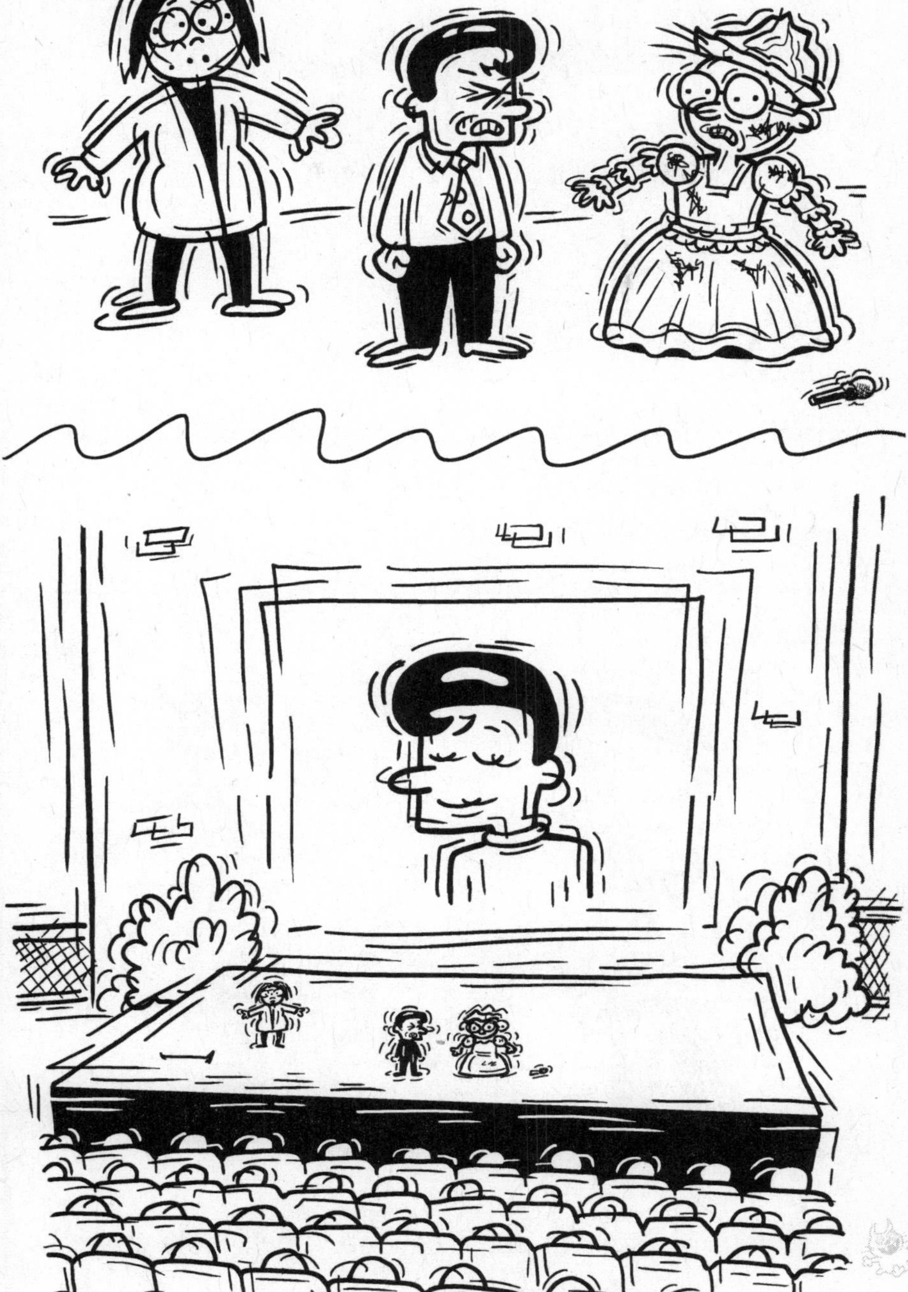

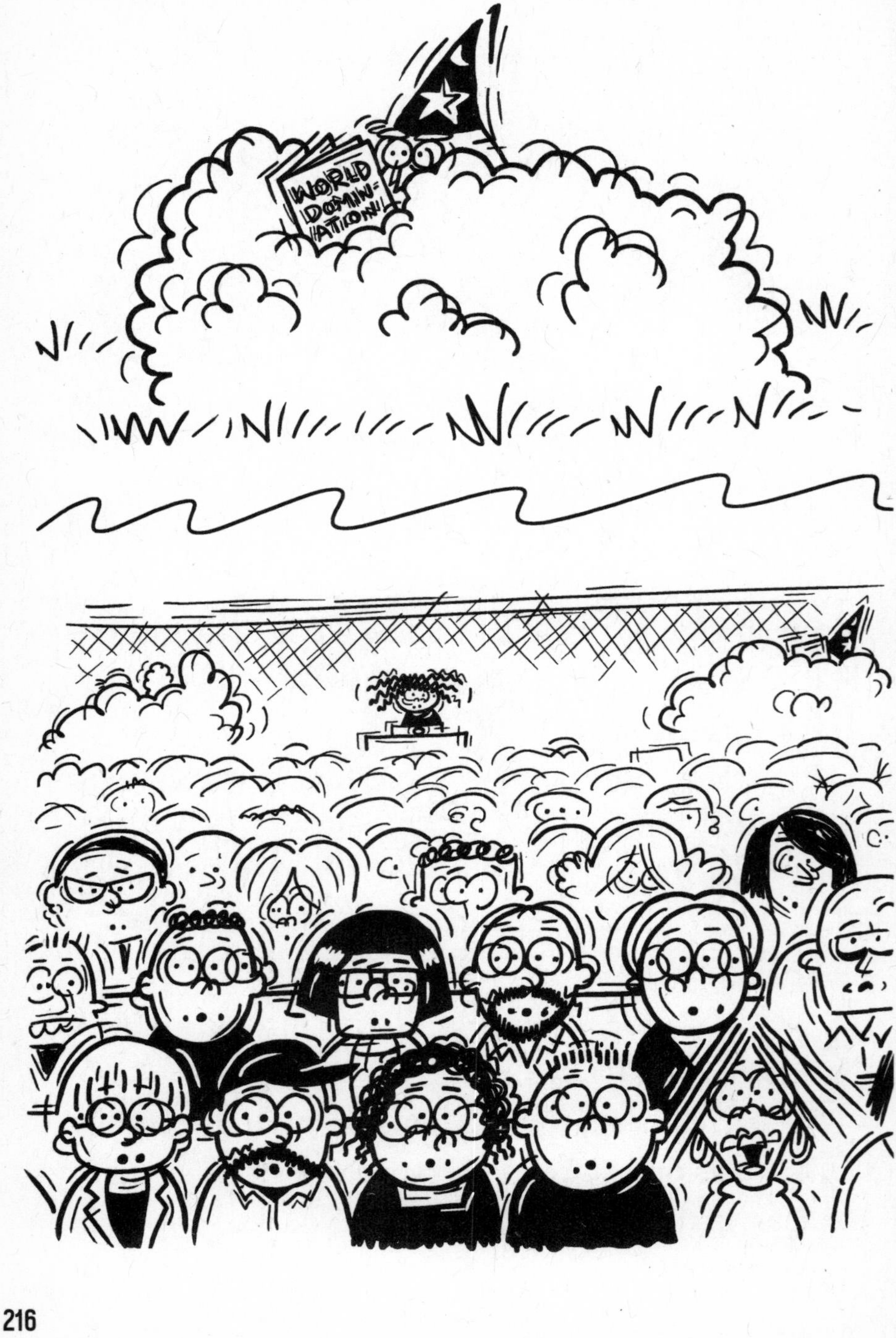
WORLD DOMIN-ATION!!

Simon is doing this! He's sending out his evil, magical brain waves! I have to protect everyone.

I pick up the mike.

"HEY, EVERYONE!" I say. "PROTECT YOURSELVES! REACH UNDER YOUR SEAT! A TINFOIL HAT HAS BEEN PLACED THERE FOR YOU! PUT IT ON YOUR HEAD!"

No one follows my instructions.

"NOW!" I yell. "PUT ON YOUR TINFOIL HATS BEFORE IT'S TOO LATE!"

Parker reaches down and puts on her foil hat. Mr. Fedora puts on his. Soon, everyone else starts doing it. And just in time!

Black magic and molten chocolate are falling everywhere. But everyone is safe.

Gurk! The mayor doesn't have a foil hat! She's completely unprotected, and it's too late to save her!

Then something comes flying out of nowhere.

Hey, I know what that is!

Now all that's left for me to do is defeat Simon once and for all!

He still looks like he's in a trance. I poke him to provoke him and say, "IT'S TIME TO ADMIT TO EVERYBODY THAT YOU'RE A WIZARD, SIMON!"

Simon snaps out of his trance and says this:

I did it! I just saved the world.

CHAPTER 43

disspelled

Everyone is safe now. Well, maybe not everyone.

As people head home, Officer Pickels comes over to congratulate me.

"Wow! I don't know how you did all that, Marty," he says. "But that was the most exciting performance art I've ever seen!"

Then Granny Pants comes over.

"Yowza, Martin! That was totally wacky packages! I knew you'd do something cockamamie!"

"Thanks for putting the foil hats under all the seats, Granny Pants! I couldn't have saved the world without you!"

"More fun than I've had in decades, Martin," she says. "I'm just amazed I could bend down low enough."

"And sorry for ruining your wedding dress," I say. "It's a mess."

"Nonsense, Martin! You look fabulous!"

Then Parker comes in for a high five, but at the last second she fakes me out and switches things up.

"You can relax," I tell her. "The magic is gone."

"I don't know about that," she whispers in my ear. "I can feel a little magic happening right now."

"So you were undercover the whole time, Parker?"

"Yup!"

"Why didn't you tell me?"

"I didn't want the secret to get out."

"Thanks for helping save the world, Parker."

"You have the best adventures, Marty!"

Uh-oh. Erica is heading my way. She's going to make fun of me. She likes to ruin my moments.

"That Simon is such a TOOL!" she says.

Simon's love spell is obviously broken.

"Marty," Erica says, "I can't believe you actually went onstage and did that ridiculous stuff in front of all those people. That took guts!"

I may have guts, but I don't have the heart to tell her it wasn't her antiwizard instructions that defeated Simon.

It was Simon who defeated Simon.

All his evil magic disappeared the moment he said this:

Once he declared that he was NOT a wizard, he magically made it come true. He made himself NOT a wizard.

I tricked him into using his own magic powers against himself. Fighting fire with fire. That's how you defeat a wizard.

LOCAL BOY SAVES DAY

Marty Pants

When The Candy Factory sprayed molten chocolate into the air, local hero Marty Pants saved everyone's bacon by supplying foil hats. "It wasn't just me who saved the day," Marty said. "It took teamwork."

There was only one injury. A man was hit in the head by a flying backpack and developed amnesia.

"I thought I had an important, sinister plan to take over something," the man said, "but now I forgot what it was."

Forgetful Man

In a related story, a citizen with a peach-fuzz mustache com-

Citizen

plained that his face was eaten by a wild dog.

He was rushed to the emergency room, where he received a series of very painful rabies shots. "Owch! Pleez! Knot again!" said the citizen.

CHAPTER 44

this must be the place

Granny drives us home. Everything seems to be back to normal inside the house.

But the place is kind of a mess. Is this what happens after a house travels through time?

And look who's back!

Granny explains the evening's events to my parents. She even adds her own exciting details.

The part of the story my parents seem to understand is that Monkey Washer Man was MINE ALL ALONG. And that I'm not expelled from school anymore.

"Marty was EXPELLED FROM SCHOOL?!" my mom says angrily to my dad. "How? When? Why didn't you TELL me?!"

"Um, er . . ." my dad mumbles. "I . . . meant . . . to. . . ."

Dad's in trouble. Time for me to save his bacon.

I stand in between them and say, "I know I do things that can be hard to understand sometimes, but deep down I know you both believe in me."

Now everyone's happy.

Granny gives me a wink and heads home. I guess I really do connect with her.

"Marty, I think you take after your granny," my mom says. "She calls herself Mini. Maybe I should call you Mini II."

Meanwhile, my dad starts cleaning up. He fixes the window with more duct tape. He's in such a good mood, he even helps me clean my room.

Wow! I didn't know the carpet was blue.

And guess what? My dad even fixed my beanbag of solitude!

Duct tape is good for anything.

"Marty, I think I know why Jerome ripped your beanbag apart," my dad says. "Somehow *this* got inside it."

I guess we'll never know how it got in there.

Erica's been whistling a lot lately. All week, in fact. She got her drone back at the ceremony, so she didn't get a zero on her science project after all. She got something a little better.

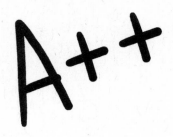

So she's pretty happy. Meanwhile, I need to find a place on my wall to hang this.

CHAPTER 45

the office

On Monday, Simon and I are called into Cricklewood's office. But this time, things go a little differently.

"Simon," Cricklewood says. "Read your apology to Marty."

I ask Cricklewood if she wants to apologize first, for expelling me for no reason.

"Just kidding," I say.

Ms. Cricklewood smiles and says, "Very charming, Marty." She's not so bad.

Simon apologizes. He even admits he was envious of my artistic skills.

"But I don't appreciate being called a monkey washer," he grumbles.

Cricklewood turns to me and says, "Marty, do you have anything you'd like to say to Simon?"

"I'll stop calling you a monkey washer," I say.

I figure now that my Monkey Washer Man cartoon is going to be a candy commercial, it'll be cool to be called a monkey washer.

But I absolutely refuse to apologize for vanquishing Simon's wizarding powers, and he doesn't bring it up.

Not only that, Simon has to give me my CACA back!

We shake hands and agree to continue loathing each other like normal.

break the cycle

And can you guess who got fired from his job at The Candy Factory?

PUNT!

Turns out Peach Fuzz was spitting on the floor. That's against company policy.*

He also deleted security footage without permission and lied about his age to get the job.

How do I know all this? I was told by the *new* security guard at The Candy Factory.

*And gross.

And since Roonie's mother is working again, he doesn't have to move away!

I ask Roongrat what he thinks of his hero, Simon, now.

"This certifiably proves Simon's a great artist!" Roongrat says.

"What? How can you say that, Roonie?"

"I read somewhere that good artists borrow, but great artists steal."

As usual, Roongrat's brain makes no sense.

On my bike ride home, I start to think about my own brain.

I decide to test my brain functions to see if I'm 100% free from black magic. I grab a pencil and try to do something I've never done before.

I DID IT!*

* But it took me three days, so I don't think I'll ever try that again.

239

CHAPTER 47

meatball

Before bed, I look at Jerome and he has that mysterious note in his mouth again. But since the black magic is gone, it doesn't say "NOWIS" anymore. It's back to saying "SIMON."

It's easy to figure out what "SIMON" stands for:

Simon
Is
Magic?
Obviously
Not!

Jerome swallows the note. It feels good knowing things are back to normal. No one has any control of my mind. No one.

Excuse me, I have to give Jerome some tuna.

I'm finally positive no one is manipulating me in any way.

Hold on, I need to give Jerome some ham.

I'm a noticer, so I would definitely notice if anyone had any power to make me do things.

Pardon me, I have to brush Jerome. And give him some vanilla ice cream. And some sausage. And some sliced turkey.*

* And a meatball.

CHAPTER 48

and in the end

The excitement is over. What now?

I suppose I could read a book.

Or redo that math homework.

Or clean my room.

I have no idea how my room got messy again so fast.

I decide to go to bed.

This will be the best night's sleep I've had in days.

There are no earth-shattering dangers to deal with.

No mysterious notes in Jerome's mouth.

Just normal kid stuff.

Yup.

That's how I like it. Slow and boring.

Yup. Wait!

Is that another mysterious note I see in Jerome's mouth?

No, I guess not. My mistake.

But just to be safe, I better check again soon.

Like in the morning.

Or every fifteen minutes.

THE END

Praise for the Marty Pants series

"Both text and art deliver zingers and running gags
that will keep kids laughing."
—*Publishers Weekly*

"*Off the Mark* cartoonist Parisi's
prose-and-cartoon series kickoff is a winner."
—*Kirkus Reviews*

"Shows uncommon mastery of the Wimpy Kid genre
and narrative style. Gags and misadventures aplenty."
—ALA *Booklist*

"An easy pick for reluctant readers."
—*School Library Journal*

"Plenty of random, laugh-out-loud moments."
—YA Books Central

"Clever, fast-paced, and hilarious."
—Dav Pilkey, author of *The Adventures of Captain Underpants*
and *Dog Man*

"Marty Pants will have you laughing from the first page!"
—Jeff Kinney, author of *Diary of a Wimpy Kid*

"Funny and engaging. Marty Pants is a surefire hit!"
—Lincoln Peirce, author of *Big Nate*

About the Author

After many odd jobs and a graphic design degree, Mark Parisi created the *Off the Mark* comic panel in 1987. It is now syndicated to more than one hundred newspapers around the country, and has won the Best Newspaper Panel Award from the National Cartoonists Society three times. Mark has also won the award for Best Greeting Cards. Find Mark's cartoons at www.offthemark.com. Marty Pants is his debut novel series, and there's more fun at www.martypants.com. Mark lives in Massachusetts and is most likely covered in cat fur.